THE TROUBLE WITH BLONDIE

KARY JANE HUTTO

To my amazing family who always love me and support me no matter what!

CONTENTS

CHAPTER ONE

Today's an "I miss my daddy," kind of day. I can't believe it's already been nearly three years. Sometimes I can feel his presence near me. It's crazy. Other times, it feels like he's been gone for ten years. My heart is mending. Slowly. I'll always miss him. I'll always think of him. Obvi. But some days my heart hurts more than others. Today is a hurty-heart day.

My crazy thoughts that never stop their continuous swirling in my mind are interrupted as I just happen to look up from my book, that I obviously wasn't even concentrating on, to see *her* walk, no, no, not walk—rather, saunter and sashay through the door of the classroom. Oh, my gosh! Oh, please not another Blonde-Clone-Girl! You know the type, girls who legit look like a plastic doll. The dolls that are tall, tan, thin, and OF COURSE have the most beautiful long, blonde hair? Yeah. THAT TYPE.

I watch her saunter into MY classroom. She is stick-thin and has deeply bronzed skin. Argh! I want to hurl. Then as she's walking, I see her lanky, perfectly shaped legs. Oh, and she is dressed to the nines in a short denim mini, pink platforms, and a super teeny, tiny, skin-tight pink shirt. And her face. Perfect. Flawless. Smiley. Blue eyes. I think one of her teeth actually sparkled like in those silly gum commercials. I feel like I am standing in Target right in the middle of the pink Clone-Girl doll aisle—she is EXACTLY like a plastic doll.

No lie.

"Oh, puhleeze," I snort at no one in particular. "Gotta be a Cali transport, no doubt. Probably as 'deep as her tan,' and her tiny, pink shirt, too." It comes out kinda squeaky and very sarcastic. Which is definitely intentional.

"Oh, come on! Don't be so harsh, Gracie. She may be surprisingly different," retorts Clara in "Clone Girl's" defense.

"HA! There is NO WAY she's different. They're all the same: clones. Mean. Rude. Selfish. Boy stealers. And the list goes on."

"Gracie, come on! She could be one clone girl, as you call them, that IS different!"

"Pfff-not a chance!" I sneer. "Not. A. Chance."

Clara Benton is my best friend, has been since the second grade when she moved from Ohio to Texas. She was put at the same table where I was, and the rest is history, as they say. Usually, we see eye to eye on most everything, but *not* when it comes to Blonde-Clone-Girlie types. I just can't stand them and yes, I'm being very cliche and judgmental. Very. And I am unapologetic about being so judgy. I couldn't care less.

"Yeah, right! They are all the same. Shallow. Stupid. Stuck-up. Only know how to shop, apply ridiculous amounts of make-up, hang all over guys, and overall just dumb," I retort to the air around me.

Clara rolls her eyes at me and turns toward the front. I smirk since I feel content with myself in my summation of "Blonde-Clone-Girl," and turn to my book to pick up where I left off before I was ruminating in my feel-sorry-for-myself mind swirl AND being *rudely* thrown off by the entrance of Blondie. AND to top it off in my smugness and coinciding reading/musing, I miss seeing Clone Girl approach the teacher's desk and miss seeing him point her in MY direction—to the desk right in front of me. It is only when her long, blonde hair sweeps over my desk and pages that I can't help but take notice.

"Do you mind, Blondie?" I growl through clenched teeth.

"Oh, I'm *so* sorry, really, I am! And, um, hi! My name is Brooke." She smiles cheerfully at me and extends her perfectly manicured, tiny hand.

"I think I'm gonna hurl." I enunciate these words under my breath, but just loud enough for her to hear, give her a fake smile, and go back to my book. And no, I don't shake her hand.

"Blondie" looks at me, smiles, and whips her head around, once again brushing my desk and my book's pages with her…. Wait, what did it smell like? Coconut? Maybe, mango? Whatever scent it is, it's wafting up my nose and I can't help but become deeply acquainted with her very long and luxurious, blonde hair that smells ridiculously amazing.

Mr. McFadden calls us to order to start another lovely day of Language Arts. Frankly, I've never been so happy to start class since I was spared any further dialogue with Blondie. We've been studying poetry. Mary Oliver in particular. She is literally an amazing author.

Today we are to partner up and discuss the poem I WORRIED by Mary Oliver. Guess who I am partnered with? Blondie. Of course. Ew.

Mr. McFadden has each of us take a copy of the poem. Then we are to read it to ourselves. Then again, then make some notes and observations then discuss it. And this is how our discussion begins with Brooke being an airhead right from the start.

"Well, what exactly is she worried about?" Brooke looks at me with a blank stare.

"She tells us in the poem." I roll my eyes. Duh.

"Yeah, but it's not like she can control any of those things anyway."

"Exactly."

"But why is she saying she's worried about those things?" she asks.

Oh, my. I'm going to lose my mind. "So-and this is just my own humble opinion-she's saying it is pointless to worry, like you said, and she lists all of those things that are out of our hands to worry about and realizes she can do whatever she puts her mind to, and that worrying is a waste of time."

"Oh."

And that is it. We pull our desks back into place and have a riveting group discussion. I am eating it all up. I love poetry so much!

❧

BELLS RING. KIDS WALK. CLASSES CHANGE. ANOTHER START TO A GREAT day of high school. I'm being obviously sarcastic. Please! I can't wait to graduate! Okay, that's a little dramatic. Maybe I'm at least ready for our next break, ha ha!

I manage to avoid Blondie in the hallway, and I always sit by Clara in choir, so phew! I survive the day with Blondie in our school now.

Right now, I'm in my junior year at Madras High, in a southern Texas city called Katy. I've been in Texas for my whole life, and I love it here. I'm cruising through my life just fine. Have good friends. In choir. Busy with my schoolwork. I work at the local pizza place. I'm set.

I'm not the most popular, but I find myself sitting comfortably right in the middle, a safe enough position to be in. This position offers me social interaction and time to get good grades. That's why, when I see Blondie today, it ticks me off. Why? Because those kinds of girls tend to mess things up for the rest of us non-Blonde-Clone types. They are beautiful, so all of our guy friends ogle over them. It's disgusting. Even guys who don't ogle over pretty girls on a daily basis become mesmerized and lose all aptitude to act normal. They lose all perspective and reality. Seriously.

It already happened our freshman year when little Miss-pretty Amanda moved in. We are a small town and a small school, so everyone knows everyone and everything. Typical little town culture, too. Freshman year, Amanda moves in from Florida to our small town, and our small school. She is tall, blonde, thin as a rail, and snotty. Oh, man! Was she snotty! And so dumb. She became the Pied

Piper of Madras High, and we other Skipper types watched as our once long-time guy friends lost their ever-loving minds!

In fact, my best friend Justin went "to the dark side," as I call it, and fell head over heels for Amanda. Of course, she broke his heart. I mean squished it. Dead. It took him a year to recover. And during that year, I was his therapist.

He and I hung out a lot. I mean a lot, a lot. We became much closer as friends. In fact, I'd say Justin became like a brother to me. It's a good thing we hung out together because he was a wreck for about six months, then the other six months he slowly came out of his slump. He gained more confidence and muscles—as did I—because we ended up becoming members of a fitness club located in the middle of our houses.

It was actually great. He and I "worked out" physically any and all aggressions and anger we had pent up inside of us. Alas, just as Justin was coming out of his heartbroken state, it was around the time my dad died. Justin kept going to the gym. I was too sad, but also, we had to cut back on expenses, so I had to quit the gym.

Justin kept going and still does. It was his soul saver, and it still is. I ended up running outside and doing yoga in my room. I still do this at least a few times a week. The yoga was actually my soul saver like the gym was for Justin. I don't know why. It was just a quiet time, I guess. Time for me to reflect. To mourn. To digest. If ever I am stressed I put on a YouTube yoga video and do it. It's so good for me!

Anyways, Justin recovered. He's even better and is super fit and confident. And he's been very cautious with pretty girls.

Luckily for all of us, Amanda moved away the summer before sophomore year. Thank the Texas stars!

So, when I see "Blondie" today, all of those painful memories flood my entire brain and remind me of freshman year, and how upset Justin was and how wrecked he was. Ugh.

In my opinion, and this is strictly my true and honest opinion, most beautiful girls are shallow and snotty. The girls just KNOW they are beautiful and play upon that for all it's worth. I, on the other hand, try to just keep myself well-kept, wear simple make-up, and have a decent, casual yet feminine wardrobe and try to keep out of others' way.

This formula aids me mucho, and I get along just great.

Okay, I just need to do a little more ranting. The worst thing about a Blonde-Clone-Girl type is the way every guy AND even girl reacts to her beauty. They literally worship her, plus will do *anything* for her. What then? What about us regular girls who are pretty enough and have actual brains in our heads? Anyone? Hello? Bueller?

After first period when I think the fun can't possibly continue for me any further, I soon discover that I have the unfortunate privilege of having "Blondie" in two of my other classes—math and choir. Ugh.

I sigh each time I see her, and she just waves and smiles. Seriously? This week is going to be *very, very long*. Luckily, there aren't any open seats for Blondie girl to even sit remotely close to me in choir, plus I sit by Clara, like I said, and it's the same in math, so SAVED.

But I do have the advantage of sitting far enough away so I can watch her flit, saunter, flirt, and just overall be absurd and ridiculous! Honestly.

She has got to be legit exhausted after a day in her life!

CHAPTER TWO

I am reviewing the day as I drive Old Blue, my pick-up, home. I am not looking forward to tomorrow, nor really any day with Blondie in it! Good grief. Just when I am so content and comfortable with my life-for once, in walks Blondie.

"She's like a boomerang," I say. "Just when I think she's not around, she pops up out of nowhere and comes right back to me. Doesn't she get it? I. Don't. Like. Her. Type. And. I. Never. Will. And this is not going to change, like ever. I'm def not going to try to be friends either. That is never gonna happen." I tell Old Blue all of my woes. Poor truck. He is such a good listener, ha ha!

"Ah, there it is!" I think to myself as I turn into my driveway.

My sweet, little, humble, yellow house! It is such a wonderful place for me to rejuvenate after a long day amongst the "wolves." I run up the stairs quickly and push open the front door. I grab a snack and change. I have approximately seven minutes to do all this and get out the door to work, and not be late.

My mom is in her office, which is right off of the kitchen. I call out to her. "Going to work, Mom! Be home by 8 pm!"

"Bye! See 'ya tonight, Gracie!"

I pull open the front door, jump down the three steps, start up Old

Blue, check my mirrors, and pull out. Good thing I live close to both school *and* work, or I could never cut it this close. And I need to mention here that it is a good thing I have an awesome mom. I mean, I know most teens don't really say that and all, but with all that has happened over the last few years—Dad dying and all—she's even more stellar.

My mom's a writer. She's published tons of books. She's actually a really great writer, too. Not just saying this 'cause she's my mom, either. She really is very talented.

Most days, I can hear her typing as I enter the house. Deadlines require even more furious typing if she's going to get paid. It does require a substantial amount of moolah to feed and clothe three kids and herself, especially with all three kids being teens.

Mom makes decent money, but it comes in spurts, and thankfully, we had a substantial life-insurance policy on my dad, so that came through after he died. But even still, those of us able to work, do. That means my mom, my brother Zac, and myself.

So let me tell you a bit more about myself and my siblings. My real name is Grace Ann Miller, but somewhere along the way I start being called Gracie, and it stuck. I don't mind so much. It fits me. It's a simple nickname for a simple girl.

I am named after my great grandma on my Dad's side. Great-grandma Grace Ann was a stubborn and strong-willed person. Just like I am. I loved when dad would tell me about his grandma and her crazy stories, like when a rattlesnake got into her field where she was working, and she casually chopped off its head with her hoe, and kept on working. Love that determination and strength and her no-nonsense attitude.

Zac—what can I say other than he's cool, smart, kind, responsible, and the bestest big brother ever. We're fifteen months apart, so he's a senior. He's had a girlfriend—Sarah—for almost two years now. She's the same way—kind, smart, and responsible. They're actually a great couple together. Wouldn't surprise me one bit if they got married down the road.

Zac works at Golf-n-Go. He loves it! Which is good since he's worked there since he was sixteen. Since we are so close in age, he and I are to share Grandpa Ben's old, blue truck while he's saving his money for college, and for his own car. He wants a Tundra truck. Shocker! What he doesn't save, he spends on his PYT—his girlfriend, Sarah. Luckily for me, Sarah's family is banked, so I always get the truck since his girlfriend has an extra car or two to spare. What would that be like? Pft! I'm actually pretty grateful since I love Old Blue.

Beth is the youngest and in eighth grade now. And she's just the sweetest. Also, super smart. She'll def go far in life for sure! She's in a lot of accelerated classes, so schoolwork is abundant for her. Luckily, she loves it. She typically has a few friends who come around a few times per week for some study sesh's. She's also in choir and plays field hockey.

As I drive to work, I numb my thought-filled brain with my current Spotify playlist. After a long and grueling day at high school, music just hits the spot for me. Between my yoga and my playlist, I am able to "rest and digest," as my therapist is always recommending I do.

I pull into the "Magnolia Place," the strip mall. In Texas, and the south in general, magnolia trees are a big thing. I find a parking spot and guide Old Blue in. Old Blue's driver side door squeaks as I open it and jump down out of my truck. I grab my phone and shove it into my backpack. I close the door, listening to more squeaking, and walk toward "Sicily's Take and Bake Pizza."

I have worked here for almost two years. It's the best place to work ever—great pizza, great people. It's a take-and-bake pizza place, as the name says, ha ha. You order what you want and take it home and cook it. We've eaten there for years, so I was totally happy when I got hired on last year, and the owners are my favorite part of Sicily's —kind and hard-working, and my friends.

"Hey guys!" I exclaim, entering my second home.

I love working at Sicily's. The staff is hard-working and supportive. My good friend is Julie, who also happens to be my manager. She and her husband, Shawn, own Sicily's Take and Bake Pizza Palace.

They hired a group of teens to run their business. Me and a guy named Joe make the pizzas. Shawn and Julie oversee. Jeff and Kelly run the register. Travis does all the other odd jobs. We get a lot of business, since this is the only take-and-bake place around.

"Hey, back, Gracie. How was school today?"

"Oh, just fabulous!" I retort sarcastically. "Boring classes, cliquish groups, drama, homework, you get the gist. What more can I say?"

"Can't say I miss those days!!" Julie snort-laughed.

"Oh, come on now, you know you're *super* jealous!"

Julie continues to laugh, which causes her soft blue eyes to light up even more. Julie is tall, with naturally curly, dark, brown hair, and she's very slender, except for the growing bulge around her middle. She's due with their third and last child, but still has a few more months to go, even though she looks as if she is going to give birth sooner. Poor thing!

My typical weeknight shift is from five to eight pm, so I can have time at night to complete my homework. I work two nights per week, and then a long shift on most Saturdays. Sicily's Take and Bake Pizza Palace is always busy, so my shifts usually fly by, even on the weekdays, though it can be a bit less busy than the weekends, but still busy by most anyone's definition of what busy looks like.

Most shifts, I'm so busy working hard, having fun, and laughing along the way that I literally never remember to take a break at all, or barely look up from the pizza-making area. Ditto for tonight's shift. Before I know it, it is nearly closing time, and there are just a few customers lingering as they await their orders.

"Finally, it's almost closing time—woohoo!" I say cheerfully as I run to the restroom and get some water to drink.

I walk quickly back to my post, and I hear the door chime ring. And as déjà vu tends to work, I look up just in time to see the very one and only new Blonde Clone Girl walk through the door. I groan to myself. It must be louder that I realize, 'cause Joe has a questioning look on his face as he turns toward me. I want to run away as I hear the words come out of her mouth.

Too. Late.

"Oh, hey, Gracie! It's Brooke, remember me? I sit in front of you in Language Arts today?"

"How could I forget, *you're as pretty as a flower*," I mutter in a high-pitched sassy tone, but way under my breath.

"Um, what? Did you say something?"

"Oh, I just said, um, what can I get for you tonight?"

"Oh, uh, a, um, a large pepperoni pizza please."

"Okay," I sigh, "I'll make your pizza. You go to the register and pay and then come and get it down here." I point, all the while fake-smiling, hoping not to have my face display a look of annoyance that I for real was feeling from my head to my toes.

"Okay, thanks." Drippy, sugary sweet voice and smile. Ew.

Clone pays, and I hand her the pizza. "Do you know how to cook it?" I ask, trying to hide the potential vomitous feeling I have in my throat.

"No, actually, not at all. Sorry."

"Put it on 425 for 12-15 minutes. Pop the bubbles. Voila."

"Oh! Gracie! You speak French? Oh, me too! *Parfait!* Okay, thanks. See 'ya tomorrow!"

Do I speak French? Is she for real? I grumble to myself.

And off she flits. Her and her tan-tall-self saunters out the door, leaving behind a trail of sweet-scented perfume.

"Ugh." That is all I can say.

"So, you know her, Gracie?" Jeff says, drooling all over himself.

"No. She just sits in front of me in class, and maybe she's in a few of my other classes, but no. We're not friends, actually barely acquaintances, to be honest. That's all. She's new, just moved here," I say with obvious disdain.

"She's gorgeous! You just gotta introduce me!"

"Yeah, yeah, okay. Another day, maybe? I gotta go. See 'ya Julie, Shawn, fellow workers!" I smile and give a Princess Diaries wave while I push the door open.

Julie peeks her head out from the back room as I hold the door open. "Thanks for your hard work, Gracie. See you Thursday for more tons of fun!"

I wave and smile as the door creaks closed. I sigh a content sigh. "Another great night. I really like Julie and Shawn. They are amazing to work for. I couldn't ask for a better job," I whisper to myself as I walk a satisfied yet distracted walk to the truck and reach out to open up the door to my grandpa's old midnight blue pick-up. I yawn. My tiredness is starting to settle into my weary-teenage bones. All I can think about right now is getting home and stretching out for a bit.

I buckle, check all my mirrors, put the truck into reverse, step on the gas pedal, and slowly back out…

"CRUUNNCH!"

CHAPTER THREE

I slam on my brakes! Hard!

"What the—?" I say really loudly! I turn to see a red mustang behind me.

"Crap. Crappity crap! No, no, no-Just what we DO NOT need. This is gonna cost us so much money that we probably don't have. Gosh dangit! I can't believe it!!" I yell aloud as I start to tear up, but quickly stop myself and like a sloth in a tree, I slowly crawl out of my car.

And there is Blonde Clone girl.

"You have GOT to be kidding me!" I mumble, loudly and angrily.

"Oh dear! I didn't see you when you were pulling out. I am sooooo sorry and now, I'm gonna be SOOOO dead!" She puts her beautiful face in her tiny, perfect hands and begins to sob, softly. Her blonde hair cascades down around her like a Hawaiian waterfall.

"Oh, please," I groan softly to myself. "She even cries prettily? Is that even possible?"

She doesn't stop crying, and I stand there looking like a statue. Good grief. I decide I better say something, and not just stand here like a freaky statue girl.

"Hey, um, Brooke, right? Hey, no big deal. Let's check the cars, see if there's any real damage and get on our way. Okay?" I try to say these words in the sweetest voice I can muster up. It doesn't come naturally. Trust me. Sounds more robotic than anything.

"Okay," Brooke softly whispers.

I check my truck first. Looks okay. Sweet. No damage. And then I look up and see a huge dent in her shiny, red mustang. I cringe.

"Well," Clone sniffs. "It is probably my fault, so let me give you my insurance info for your mom or dad to call," she says. "I'm dead meat, even if it isn't my fault, because according to my dad, *everything* is my fault. He thinks I'm just a dumb blonde…" Her pain-filled voice trails off into the now crisp, surrounding air. And as she's blubbering out her words.

All I'm thinking to myself is, "Woah, woah, slow down Blondie, let's not start a therapy session here. I just want to go HOME."

Finally, I muster up some niceness.

"Hey, Brooke, if it makes you feel any better, I'm just as dead. And, it probably is MY fault, too. Money is tight at my house. My mom and brother and I all work to make ends meet, so this news will not be taken lightly."

I sigh. Brooke exhales out a sigh, too. We exchange info and then we both reluctantly gather our wits and drive to our separate homes, if only to reap our just reward for our mistake. Brooke waves sadly as she leaves the parking lot. I actually have a very teeny, tiny tinge of care and concern wash over me for a small moment. Then I immediately get over it, but my thoughts sure don't….

"Clone girl will be fine," I voice aloud to my steering wheel. "Her type always is. Plus, her daddy's probably loaded, so she won't feel any financial sting whatsoever. Pa-thet-ic," I reassure myself as I grouchily putter out of the parking lot.

But, then of course, all of the worried thoughts about how my mother is going to react begin to crowd out anything pleasant at the time being and I just feet, well, grumpy.

Rounding the corner, I see my cute yellow house first, then I see there is still a light on in the kitchen. That means Mom is in her room. Good. I pull in and park Old Blue. I step out into the crisp air once more and approach the front door with a bit of trepidation.

"Crap. I so don't need this stress, and neither does Mom, actually," I growl disgustedly before I open the front door. I grit my teeth and take three deep breaths—therapy tool for the win!

I slink into the kitchen and wash my hands in the sink. Slowly—I feel like I'm having an out-of-body experience—I grab an apple and some cheese sticks and start up the stairs. I then wander down the hallway in slow-motion. I attempt to count to 100 in my head to calm myself (another technique—ha ha!). I can hear the television humming in my mother's room. My poor mom. She has slept with the telly on every night since my dad passed away. Makes her feel less lonely, she had told us all on a few occasions. Can't say I blame her.

"Mom, you awake?" I carefully open her door and peek in.

"That you Gracie? Come on in, hon'."

I enter her room with soft, labored steps.

"How was work sweetie?" she asks sleepily.

"Great, as always," I answer back quickly. Then I think to ask her a question so I can get to my room before she uses her mother-sixth-sense and reads the guilt on my face.

"So, hey, how'd the writing go tonight? And where are Zac and Beth?" I continue to put on an air of confidence, even though I'm terrified inside.

"Zac is with Sarah "studying." She uses her hands and makes air quotes. "And Beth is in her room finishing up her PowerPoint project."

"Okay, great. Well, I better get on with my homework." I check my watch and realize it is nearly nine pm.

"Well, okay. So, work was good? Anything exciting happen?" Mom tends to repeat things when she's tired, so I nonchalantly answer her again.

"Nope! Same ol' same oh! Just great. Love my job! Anything exciting happen here at the house?"

"Uh, nope, not a thing. Business as usual." Mom is eyeing me weirdly, but I just keep talking.

"Okay, so cool. Well, I really gotta get started on the ol' HW, Mom. See 'ya in the morning."

"Good night, sweetie."

"Love you, Mom."

I walk out as quickly as I can and quietly close my mom's door. I can't do it. I can't tell her, not yet. "I will tomorrow," I whisper to myself as I walk to my room. "Yeah right, who am I kidding?"

I fling my crossbody and my phone onto my bed and then myself, and I grab my notebook and jot down a few thoughts. It's another great therapy technique—I write daily if I can.

"1. What a day! A new bimbo in my class.

2. Blonde, stupid, shamefully pretty and tan!

3. And as if that isn't enough? I rammed my car into her precious car! Why is she already torturing me?"

I hustle through my homework and bedtime routine, and grab my kindle. A little reading always helps me to sleep quickly, which I do almost immediately.

I see my therapist, Cindy, nowadays just when I need to after school. I started about a year after dad died. My brain just needed help. I look forward to it. It helps me to deal with the many emotions I continuously have about my dad.

And now with Blondie! Argh! I will need to talk this all out with Cindy at my appointment on Thursday.

PHEW! I MAKE IT TO THURSDAY. BUT BARELY! THANKFULLY, I AM able to talk out all of my feelings about Brooke. I can't even handle the way she is. I can't handle *who* she is, what she represents. Just reminds me of our freshman year. And it reminds me that I'm just insignificant because of how I look, which I know is ridiculous. But it's how I feel when I'm around girls like Blondie.

Luckily, I'm able to talk this out with Cindy, and am able to get some ideas to help me cope with the situation. I tell her all about

Brooke—and that I call her Blondie—and how I'm terrified she will be just like all the other clone girls I've known in my life.

Cindy tells me to write these thoughts into my journal. Every event. Every experience. I'm always grateful for my therapist.

"COCK-A-DOODLE-DOO! COCK-A-DOODLE-DOO! COCK-A-DOODLE-doo!"

"Noooo! Not already! Uuuggghhh."

Nooooooooo! That freakin' alarm clock! TOO SOON! But, I have to get up, so I swing my legs over the side of my bed. My vision is still blurry by a lack of sleep, but I drag myself over to my alarm clock. I slam down the button and amble into the bathroom.

Two days have passed, and I still haven't told my mom about the car incident. My mind is still thinking about that when the alarm goes off AGAIN. That blasted rooster crow gets louder and louder each time it blares out of the clock until you physically turn it off.

I am not feeling very spry today. I can't believe I have to go to school. Again. Grrrrrr. But, c'est la vie! And, I guess there is a pro to that stupid clock. It wakes me up, yeah, sure, but then at the same time, I want to *smash* it to smithereens.

"Wow. Lookin' good, Gracie! Nice zit on your chin," I tell my mirror. One day I for real expect it to answer back with a, "This is as good as it's gonna get, baby," like the mirror in Snow White–but my mirror will just up and break!

I glare at my reflection. Looks like another bad hair day *and* a bad face day, too. Ew.

"Oh goody! Wonder how I will be able to fix myself in time for school? Not enough time in the world to fix this mess, but at least it is Friday. Oh! At least it IS Friday! Whew! This has been one heck of a week with the whole Clone Girl moving here, being in my classes and the car crash. I need some serious R & R tomorrow. I am so glad I'm off from work and that I can hang with Clara and Justin tomorrow. We are so hitting the mall and maybe catching a movie this weekend."

I continue to talk to the mirror. I know it's sort of goofy to talk to my mirror, but it is actually very therapeutic, too!

Breakfast is my favorite meal of the day: oatmeal and toast.

"Breakfast of champions," my dad used to say every day before he… died. I swallow the knot in my throat and grab my backpack. Dad has been gone almost three years now, but it still hurts, a lot.

"Zac, Beth, you guys ready? Let's go. It's FRIDAY!"

"See 'ya, Mom!" Zac and Beth say almost in unison as they clamber down the stairs and pass me. I chime in after. I grab my backpack and shut the front door.

"Bye you guys!" Mom yells from her office.

She has been up typing early. I could hear the steady clickety-click drumming through my head. Her book is due, so she has to crank it out. Deadlines for Mom mean independent living for us. We three don't mind so much though.

Mom's head pops out of the screen door as we are about to veer out of the driveway.

"Hey guys, I'm gonna be here all day and then I'm meeting Kenneth for dessert later to go over what I have written so far. Have a great day!"

And she is gone. The typing instantly commences.

Mom types on an old typewriter. I know it sounds crazy. She just loves to hear the clickety clack of the keys as she's drumming along. Then she has Kenneth scan it all onto her laptop.

Kenneth is her editor and has been her editor for almost ten years. And as of nowadays, I'm more than positive he's a potential love-interest. Hey, my mom isn't exactly ugly. She is actually *really* pretty, for an older woman, and you know, a mom.

Kenneth had moved more into the picture pretty much right after dad died, when mom had sold her sixth novel via Kenneth's publishing company, Thompson and Sons. The move to them has proven to be a very good step both financially and now, for companionship for my mom.

She is well on her way to becoming more recognized. She is

writing her seventh installment in a possible eight to ten book young adult series. I am very proud of her.

A few years ago, I asked her what made her want to be an author. She told me she read a few books when she was younger on repeat. *The Secret Garden. The Wizard of Oz. James and the Giant Peach.* From these three books and many, many others she's read over the years, she decided she had stories to tell, too. So, from a young age, she started to keep a spiral notebook. She works so hard for us, and I know she keeps a smile on her face while around us these days, but I can hear her in her room sometimes. Her muffled sobs echo through my wall.

CHAPTER FOUR

I told Zac about Mom crying one morning a few weeks ago 'cause I could hear her, since Mom's room is right next to mine.

His face was grim but stoic and he simply said, "This is why you and I work so very hard. For Mom's sake. She's been so strong through all this."

"Yeah, agreed. I know Zac. I know. But it hasn't been easy on any of us, though," I trailed off as Zac whispered, "Yeah."

As he walked down the stairs. I was still getting ready for school when that convo broke out and then BAM! The memories flooded throughout my entire brain. There have been some very ugly, hard days since that fateful day three years ago—well, almost three years ago, when we found out that our dad had died due to injuries sustained in a car crash.

My dad was the most kind and considerate man. I'm sure he let someone through or something nice like that just before he got hit head-on. He was coming home from work—well, from downtown Houston. Regular day. Regular time. Regular traffic. But not regular people. That particular day, an older grandpa had a medical emergency—a heart attack or stroke. I'm not all the way sure. All we know from the cops telling us the details is that it was truly an accident. He blacked out and his car careened into our dad's car.

Dad had gone into Houston for a business conference and was on his way home, when an elderly man going the wrong way hit dad head-on. The grandpa died upon impact. The cops also told us that the old guy was picking up dinner for him and his wife that night. The elderly man died at the scene. I made sure I prayed for the old man's wife.

Dad was life-flighted to the nearest hospital. Mom and all of us made it with time to say good-bye to Dad. He was lucid for just a small amount of time. Enough time for me to hold his hand and cry like a baby at his bedside. Enough for him to tell me he loved me. Enough time for all of us to be gathered around an amazing man's bedside and watch his bright, shining, luminescent light go out.

All of it was gruesome and heart wrenching. For both parties. You just never know when something like this could happen. It's the strangest feeling though, when it does. Strange. Empty. Upsetting. Numbing. There are so many emotions you go through. You know those five stages of grief? Anger. Sadness. Forgiveness. Peace. And something else. Well, you go through those stages continuously. Not just when a bad event happens. Oh, no. When you least suspect it, one of those sneaky stages will slap you like when you go out the door into below zero temps. Like a solid, jarring slap on your soul and heart. I was in the eighth grade. As if being a teen in middle school isn't awkward and frustrating enough, throw in a life-changing tragedy, and things get really, really ugly!

I think time stood still for hours as we were all surrounding Dad's bed and watched as they covered him up with a sheet and wheeled him out. Mom sobbed and sobbed. Then we all sobbed and pulled each other close into a circle, hugging each other.

I kept replaying the whole horrid event over and over again. For so many months, I'd wake up covered in sweat. To say that I had had my heart physically ripped out of my body is an understatement. I was devastated. My dad was too young to die! We needed him, and yet, there we all were, alone, without Dad. It took almost two years before my night-terrors finally stopped. I never thought that would happen, nor did I think my heart could ever mend.

I'm not all the way healed, and I probably never really will be fully healed. A chunk of my heart died with my daddy....

I open my locker, grab what I need for ELAR, and do a quick walk to class.

And there she is again—Blondie. "Oh my gosh! I'm living in an actual nightmare. This is so *not* my week!"

All the painful thoughts of Clone girl, the dent in her car, not telling my mom felt like I just got hit with a rock to my chest.

And then, like a cherry on top of a sundae—and not in a yummy way—Blondie took the seat in front of me. Again. She turns her head toward me, which means her hair turns too and smacks me in the face. What am I smelling? Strawberries, mango, coconut—it was like a bowl of delish fruit! Seriously, what the freak kind of shampoo does she even USE?

"Hey, Gracie! I talked with my dad last night and he was actually not so mad at me, although he still said I need to be more careful when I drive, but anyways, he said it was both of our faults, well, I told him that, and then he said he would call your mom or dad and the insurance company. I am so glad, and so relieved . . ."

"K. Woah. BREATHE!" I cut her off as I look at her in amazement. She continues to babble. Seriously, babbling! "Hey, I didn't get a chance to tell my mom, so, uh, let me handle that and then I'll let you know. My mom is really busy with her novel. She's a writer, and she has an important deadline, okay, so just let me handle the talking with her, okay?"

"Yeah, sure. No problem. It's cool. What about your dad? Is he busy, too?"

Anddddd here it goes....

"Um, my dad died almost three years ago." I tend to always say this softly and sadly.

Andddddd, there it is.

Every time it's the same. The look. Silence. Sad puppy dog eyes.

The works. Then the comments and questions. I doubt I will ever get better at talking about this!

"I'm so sorry Gracie. I-I didn't know."

"It's fine. How could you even know that info?" Unfortunately for Blondie, I answer extremely curtly.

"Okay. Cool," she changes the subject quickly and is babbling, again, while she whips her head around, and leaves me in the wake of her fruit-laced tresses.

I keep quiet for the entire class. Well, I guess I do that anyway, but today my brain is *really* full. Better tell my mom S.T.A.T.

The day wears on, and last period is excruciatingly slow, even though I love Latin. I watch the clock.

"Tick, Tick, rrrriiinnnggg!"

"Finally!" I yell as I slither out of my chair and sprint for the door. If I have to hear any more Latin terms, I am going to hurl.

"Hey, little lady, let's take it easy." Mr. Thames, my Latin teacher, voices loudly toward me.

"Sorry, Mr. Thames. I, uh, just have to get to work quickly. I'll walk **really** slowly, I promise."

I flash him my best brown-noser smile and am out the door before he could say another word.

I decide to call my mom on my way to work. I am hoping this will lessen the blow. Boy, am I wrong.

"What? Why didn't you tell me Wednesday night? You know I would have wanted to make sure you were all right and, oh, Gracie, really. I expect more from you nowadays. You are by far my most level-headed child!"

I sigh sadly. I hate when she is disappointed in me. It's the worst!

"I'm sorry, Mom. But the upside is that Blondie—I mean Brooke— says it was both of our faults so the bill can be split!" I try to lay this on her in my schmoosiest voice possible.

"Well, we'll see. Next time you come and tell me immediately. Understand, young lady?"

"Yes, ma'am. Sorry. I gotta go mom. I'm here at work now. See 'ya after ten pm."

"Love you, Gracie."

"Love you, Mom."

I feel as dirty as mud on the bottom of my shoe after a Texas rainstorm. I am a heel–literally.

"Boy, I won't do that again!" I say aloud, entering Sicily's .

"He-yy Gracie! It's Friday. You survived another week of High School!"

"Barely, Shawn, barely," I retort sarcastically.

"What, you mean to tell me you don't think we miss all day class, boring teachers, homework, oh, and teen drama?"

"Ha, Ha, HA! You are *so* cute when you're sarcastic!"

"What are you two talking about?" Julie says with a smirky smile as she refills the cheese and pepperoni bins.

"Oh, you know, the joys of high school."

We both simultaneously roll our eyes at each other.

"Ah, yes, I believe Gracie and I were discussing that just the other day, weren't we? Well, no matter. Today is Friday and spring break starts too, so what could be better than that?"

I literally have forgotten. With Clone-girl on the scene and the fender bender, work, homework, goodness! My brain really is way too full, and it didn't help whenever I think or talk about my dad… fills my soul with deep, hurty emotions.

Julie, Shawn, and I laugh as they prepare the pizza dough, fill bins, and refill the sauce. We all take different jobs to refill the soda, napkins, the salads, soda pop, the cookie dough and dessert pizzas. Dessert pizza is my favorite! Hot, gooey s'mores pizza? Mmm, yes please. It is so delish.

My main job is to physically prepare the pizzas. I start at the far left side and put the dough on the cardboard circle, roll air holes in it, ladle on the sauce, then each of the different toppings depending on which pizza the patrons have ordered. We have a real good variety of pizza choices, plus Shawn and Julie will introduce a new pizza type every couple of months.

I look up here and there as the bell on the door chimes non-stop, and a slew of people trickle in. Some people call in advance, but most just pop in and order.

Business is crazy busy on Friday nights, starting at five pm, so we have to be as prepared as possible.

"And here they come!!" Julie says enthusiastically.

I glance up again just in time to see a few different cars pull up and more potential clients hungrily enter through the door.

I know I say this every time I work, especially on Fridays and Saturdays, BUT to say the night IS busy. My adrenaline is pumping like when I run, and I have so much energy! Plus, I don't have time to think about anything in my full brain. I laugh, I work, I clean, I work some more!

At ten pm Shawn locks the door. I text my mom to say that we closed and are doing clean-up so she doesn't worry about me. She does that kind of stuff. Worries. It's a mom thing.

Cleaning up takes a good hour and then all seven of us climb into our cars. Exhausted, but satisfied at a job well done.

I call Zac on my way home from Sicily's since I knew he would be doing the same thing: coming home from work at Golf-n-Go. Working late on a Friday night, too. We were such "party animals," he and I—ha ha!

"What's up bro?" I begin.

"Hey sis, feels like I haven't seen you for days and we live in the same house." He laughs his contagious laugh.

"Totally. It's downright ridiculous! Wanna watch a movie when we get home? That new vampire flick is out digitally, and I already bought it last weekend."

"Sounds cool. We may fall asleep, but it's worth a shot at some Friday night excitement, eh?"

"Yep. See 'ya in about ten minutes."

"K. bye, Sis!"

CHAPTER FIVE

A smile creeps across my lips and warms my heart.

"I have a very cool brother," I state happily to Old Blue.

Being close in age, we have become more than just siblings, but good friends, too. I love this. Even if he and his girlfriend Sarah are tight, he still took the time to hang with Beth and me.

Beth! Sheesh! I haven't seen her for days either! I reach the stop light just as it turns red and shoot a text to Beth to see if she wants to join us for a movie watching/falling asleep party when Zac and I get home.

"I'm in! See you in a bit, Gracie!"

It will always be my favorite thing to come around the bend and see my house bathed in the streetlight's soft glow. I see Zac's taillights as he pulls in just minutes before I do. I mean, one of Sarah's cars, with Zac in it.

And then my next thought is this. "I GET TO SLEEP IN!" I yell to Old Blue! It seems like it has been ages for both Zac and me, when in reality, it's been just one week!

"And spring break!" I yell as I slam Old Blue's door shut with glee! I skip up the walkway, up the three steps and open the front door. "I'm home!" I shout to my cutie house.

Between our eight-hour school days and our different work shifts, the weeks fly by, and respite comes few and far between for Zac and me. Even for Beth. Her schedule has cranked up this past year too, with homework and extracurricular activities. We three kiddos are on a carousel of craziness every week. So, between all three of us, lazily hanging around the home front didn't happen very often.

First things first, though—watch a movie with Zac and Beth. I microwave some popcorn for us all and grab three cups and some lemonade.

"Let's go guys! I'm queuing up the cheesy vampire movie!"

I hear Beth trample down the stairs. "I'm here!" As she plops herself on our comfy grandma couch, as we call it. It's a crazy disco-floral print, but it's literally the most comfortable couch ever.

"Here I am, too!" Zac skids into the telly room 'cause he's in his socks and the wood floor is slippery. He's so funny! He also plops himself onto the grandma couch and I hit play.

And yes, forty-five minutes into the movie, full of popcorn and lemonade and having chatted and laughed together, we totally fall asleep.

I awake to the morning sun warming me in my bed. I slowly roll over. I flutter my eyes a few times to adjust to the sunlight. Then I lazily just lay in my bed. I put on my "fave songs" playlist and continue to soak in the sun's rays and the solitude. No crowing rooster alarm. Hallelujah. Next, I check my phone. "Okay, so maybe it's not am anymore! Sheesh! It's 12:15 pm!"

Clara and Justin both had texted, and we are going to meet up in a few hours. I am stoked to hang with Clara and Justin. Seems like that hasn't happened for a long while either. Good grief! I'm only seventeen!

"Sun. Bed. No alarm clock. Smells of yumminess. It is definitely Saturday!" These calming words I share with my adorable bathroom mirror and inanimate object bestie! "Being a teen shouldn't be THIS strenuous, should it?" I smile to myself in the mirror. "Hey mirror, have I ever mentioned to you HOW much I LOVE Saturdays?"

I giggle to myself and get ready to shower and dress as slowly as possible. I actually take wayyyy more time on my hair and make-up. It feels amazing to do this. The movie starts at 1:30 pm, so I have plenty of time.

Now dressed and properly primped, I continue to rock out while I pick up my horribly neglected room. It *has* been a long few weeks. After rediscovering some clothing items I thought had been definitely snatched by Beth or even by my mom, I finally restore peace and serenity to my bedroom!

The three of us–Clara, Justin and I–plan to see a movie, eat a late lunch and do some shopping at our favorite mall—Stone Briar. I am very much looking forward to this beautiful Saturday. Very much. Zac will most likely be with Sarah, and Beth has volleyball practice and then is working on some school projects with her crew.

Beth is almost fourteen going on about twenty! The girl is a brainiac. GT. Studies all the time. Hopes to attend one of the top five colleges in the US, which will not surprise any of us when she gets into them all! She has a small group of brainiac friends and they all hang together. Well, study together, mostly.

"That girl puts us all to shame. Seriously!" I say to my mirror as I take one more look at myself. I sigh with contentment. I feel a good convo with my mirror each and every day starts me off on a good foot. Sometimes I legit wish it was magic and could grant me a few wishes maybe or even talk back to me. It was my good ol' morning companion, and I thoroughly enjoy my daily convos.

I come downstairs and chat with Mom before leaving.

"Mom, how's it going? What page are you on? When will you be done?" I smile as I ask these three questions with rapid fire.

"Woah! Slow down, child!" Mom's sarcastic tone is evident. "How about good, page 349, and hopefully by Monday?"

"Okay, now that's awesome progress, Mom. I'm very happy for you!"

"Me too! I'm telling you, this one has been a very hard novel to finish! I've had to introduce some new characters and thread them into the storyline, so it's been rather challenging. But, enough of that. So, what are you, Clara, and Justin doing today?"

"Movie, late lunch, and shopping. I'll prob be home around ten or eleven pm if that's cool with you? I'll text you throughout the day, though.

I walk to the door. "Bye everyone. Be home later," just as *These are the Days* blares from my cell. I start up my truck up, flip on the A/C, and answer, not recognizing the number

"Hello?"

"Gracie? Hey, this is Brooke."

I cringe as the melodic notes of her dulcet voice penetrate my very soul. *Not today,* I think meanly. "Hey, what's up?"

"Oh, hey, my dad talked with your mom and got everything all worked out. Not as expensive as we'd all thought. Thankfully." She giggles. "About $400 total."

"Cool, cool. So do we split the $400 then?"

"Yes. I need to take my car into the shop though, and then when it's done, we can settle up. Uh, that's the reason I'm calling. I need someone to follow me down to the repair shop and then give me a lift home. I don't really know many people. In fact, I actually know only you. Isn't that funny? So, do you think you could possibly do that?"

Ironic and hilarious. I think sarcastically to myself. *Seriously, can I NOT have just ONE day to myself. Is that too much to ask for?* I wince as I begin to answer. "Actually—" I pause and cut my own self off. "Um, yeah, I guess so. When do you need to go? I'm planning to meet some friends later today…"

"How about right now?" She laughs nervously. "I'm sorry it's late notice. My dad's out of town and my mom's getting her hair done then getting a mani/pedi, so she won't be home for a while."

"That'll work. I'm ready anyway. Do you know where Ashton Way is in the Woodlands? I'm at 2200."

"No, but I'll use Google maps and find it. Oh, you are *so* nice. Thank you! My dad said I had to get the car fixed and pay for it myself since I am the one who didn't see you."

"It's cool. See ya in a minute." I push the stop button really hard.

I text Clara and Justin. "Be there soon. Gotta do an errand or two. Save my spot, ha ha!"

I turn off my car and go back inside. I plop on the comfy sofa and wait for Blondie to arrive. I see the reflection of the sunlight bouncing off the front of the shiny red mustang as Brooke turns into our driveway. She honks her horn. I sigh.

"Here goes nothin'," I growl as I roll my eyes and I walk into the bright sunlit day, which immediately warms my grumpiness. Oh, how I love a sunny Saturday. I walk to her window.

She pushes her button and the window slides down. "Hey Gracie! If you can follow me over to the car repair place, then take me home, that would be great."

"Hey," I say with a half-smile. My heart isn't really into this little excursion, but it is the least I could do, I guess.

Why is it that sugar-coated, sweet, gushy words come out of her mouth every time it opens? Ew, so ew.

"Yeah, no problem. I've got time until I go to the mov—"

CRAP. I abruptly stop speaking.

SHOOT. TOO LATE.

"Oh, cool. So what 'cha going to see?"

"Some rom-com. Just came out. Should be mellow enough."

"Oh, fun..." Her sugary-sweet voice trails off.

Uh-oh. She wants me to invite her. I don't even have enough energy to deal with this. I hate these types of situations. Grrr.

I quickly change the subject. I'm not going to cave. Another time, maybe. But, not today. Nope!

"So where is this place?" I ask shortly.

"It says it's about ten minutes from your house. Joe's One-Stop Shop."

"Oh yeah, Joe's nice. He fixes everyone's cars around here. K. I'll meet you there." I walk to my car as Brooke closes her window, revs her engine, and peels out of my driveway.

"Is she for real? Just when I think maybe I can tolerate her a bit, she does that kind of stuff? Honestly!" It leaves a bad taste in my mouth saying all of this to myself and Old Blue as I crawl in, start the truck up, and pull out.

"Oh crap!" I spit out loudly as I realize the worst possible thing that I forgot I'd have to do! "Brooke freaking has to drive WITH ME!"

I tell myself I'd best gear myself up mentally for the ride home–in my lovely, old, blue, beat up truck. Oh joy. I crank up my radio and try to stay behind the Clone girl, watching and hoping she might get lost. She didn't, and she was at least a good driver and not a bimbo air-head like I'd expected.

She turns into Joe's One-Stop Shop. We've used him before on my pick-up. He's super good at what he does. Wonder how she knew about this place already? Well, duh, small town-big mouths is how.

I park to the side. Get out of my car and manage to catch her as she glides out of her car. She sashays into the front office. My eyes follow her every move. The chime on the door signals, and I watch as all of the workers—three guys—look up and immediately gawk and almost drool at her.

Typical dudes. Ugh.

Although even I had to admit her tan, long legs looked better than ever in her short denim skirt. No wonder they gawked. I sigh–again. She has to be almost 5'10", I guess, since I am about 5'7".

Enough. I just need to be done with this, get her home, and run away. I am not going to let this Clone-bimbo chick get into my life and steal my friends, girls and guys alike. Oh heck no.

Not again.

CHAPTER SIX

*B*londie comes out and gracefully walks toward the pickup. She pulls the passenger door open and literally slides onto the seat like she is wearing all silk. The door squeaks as it opens and shuts.

"Welcome into Old Blue," I say quickly. "'Cause it is big and blue, ha ha."

Wow. Could I be any more awkward? But I don't think she even heard me, because she immediately starts to talk once she sits down and buckles her seatbelt.

"So, it will take about two weeks. This leaves me without a car to get to school since Daddy won't let me take one of the other cars—we have five—you'd think he would let his only daughter drive at least one of them to school!" Brooke whined, but still her voice is sugary.

"Oh." That is all I can say.

I turn onto Main Street and head toward—wait, I didn't know where she lived.

"So, where am I taking you?"

"Oh, I'm so silly. Okay, you know where Principal Heights is located? I live there."

Ah, the ritzy gated community. Figures. Fits her whole persona.

Rich. Tan. Fancy, dumb, mean, and blonde. I know what you're going to say. I'm being mean.

"Sure, sure. A few of my friends live that way." We drive in silence. I push play on my rock out list. Better to have tunes, I guess, than awkward silence.

"Um, Gracie? Can I ask you something?"

Uh, oh. I mutter, "Sure…"

"I know I don't know your friends and all, um, but, um, I would really like to make some friends here. Could I come with you today? I promise I won't be any trouble. I'll keep quiet and be practically invisible."

Like that would be possible, Miss Clone Girl. She is babbling again. But what can I say to that? We are trapped in the car together. I am not *that* ruthless.

"Uh, sure. K. It's one o'clock, right, so let's just head over to the theater right now, unless you want to go by Walmart and get cheap treats to smuggle in." I laugh gingerly.

And then suddenly Clone Girl breaks into the funniest giggle-fest ever.

"Oh, Gracie. You are always so nice and funny."

I give her a goofy smile. Oh, if she could only read my thoughts, like famed vampire Edward Cullen in Twilight, she'd think otherwise AND she'd be crying like a baby.

Again, we travel in verbal silence. Thankfully, I continue to play my tunes in the background of this seriously awkward drive.

"This is our one and only Walmart! Welcome to the far east in Katy, Texas." I laugh.

I find a parking spot easily at Walmart. We walk side by side. She starts to talk about her little puppy, Sparkle, and how cute she is and how she dresses her up and has a little bag for her. I think I must have looked put out or appalled, because she stops talking for at least five minutes.

"She does like to babble," I think.

I lead her to the candy section. We pick out our favorites,

purchase them, and return to the car. Perfect 1:15pm. The theater is close by, so we are still okay.

"Um, my friend Clara and also Justin will be meeting me, well I guess now us, there. Do you know either one?"

"Oh, yes. Clara is my Chem partner, and I think Justin is in three of my classes. He is so sweet." Her beautiful face lights up. I mean she actually glows. Maybe it's her make-up, but even her hair looks blonder and shinier. Good grief! It's like she's got magic glowing through her bloodstream!

"Oh, okay, good."

And all I could think of is, Oh, I *bet* you think Justin is so nice and so sweet. He's a dude who's obsessed with you and you're gorgeous. End of story. This should be *super* fun. Just what I think will happen is going to happen. Great. All of my friends will be ogling over Clone Girl's beauty and wealth and overall amazingness, and will become her BFF's.

I sigh so loudly that Brooke turns to me and asks, "Gracie, are you okay?"

"Oh, yeah, yeah, sorry. Just ready to chill and watch a rom-com!" I laugh again as I get out of the car quickly and assertively. If I can help it, I am not going to let this Blonde Clone Girl ruin my life. Not this time… actually, I resolve to NEVER have it happen again if I can at least help it.

I text Clara and Justin as we walk in.

'Brooke is with me. Can you guys get another ticket please?'

'What? Did you get hit on the head today?? But sure.'

'V funny. Tell you later. Where are our seats located? Forgot to ask.'

'Row H 13-16.'

'Thx, coming.'

I see Clara's cute pony pops immediately as Brooke and I start up the carpeted theater steps. Justin is grabbing a handful of popcorn when he turns and sees Brooke and me coming down row H.

"Hey, Brooke, hey Gracie." Justin doesn't hide his obvious joy at seeing Brooke. I can hear it in his voice.

"Wanna sit by me, Brooke?" Justin's voice is still gleeful, and I think I could see a little sparkle in his eye. I roll my eyes but smile in spite of my annoyance with Brooke.

I settle in by Clara. We immediately start to talk about anything and everything! I swear I haven't seen her forever! Brooke sits down by me with Justin to her left. The thought crosses my mind as to WHY she's sitting by me. I don't know 'cause I've obviously shown her anything but true kindness. Whatever. I shake my head and the lights dim.

Four hours later, I am home. Besides the fact that Justin basically drooled over every word, step, and movement Brooke made, the day turns out pretty well. The movie was good, the food was great, and I found a few shirts and two skirts, so the shopping wasn't a total waste.

I am laying out my goods on my bed, snipping off the tags, and am just about to try them on and coordinate a few outfits when my brain takes my thoughts on its fave roller coaster ride of musings and ponderings, and this time, it goes to today's events and activities.

I'm admitting to myself right now that this particular Blonde Clone Girl, aka Brooke, seems different.

Maybe even tolerable… WOAH. What is happening to me? Didn't I just say earlier today that I wouldn't let anything happen to Justin or Clara, nor to me? Not now. Not ever by another blonde pretty girl? But… Brooke—though ridiculously gorgeous—is… dare I say it, for real, NICE-ISH? I shudder and giggle to myself as I continue to try on my outfits… and talk to my favorite mirror.

I shoot Clara a text before I write in my composition book and read before sleep came.

'Hey fun day right?'

'Totally fun.'

'I think Brooke is nice.'

'She's okay.'

'Come on Gracie u know she's nice.'

'Yeah I guess.'

I pull out my fave purple felt tip pen and write a few lines. "Decent day. Brooke sort of nice? Still don't trust her. But day wasn't ruined."

I like to write in free verse poetry, so I pen a few lines:

'Saturday. Free day. Sunny day. No school day. Friends. My fave. Movies. Also my fave. Shopping. My all-time favorite. Should I even entertain believing that Brooke can be trusted?'

Sleep came quickly as I sleepily mull over my thoughts....

I arise a whole lot earlier than yesterday (Saturday). I dress quickly for church and then skip down the stairs happily. I really love Sundays because we are all home together and in one place!

I cruise into the kitchen and see that Beth is all ready for church and has begun eating her breakfast.

I sit at our cozy kitchen table after preparing a few pancakes and some milk for breakfast. We have a little nook with a table and chairs. We had it painted a light, buttery yellow after Dad passed. It was one of his favorite colors.

"Cute outfit, Gracie," Beth articulates in her cute, little brainiac voice.

"Thanks, Beth! Picked it up yesterday while I was shopping with Clara, Justin, and Brooke."

"Brooke? Who's that?"

"Some new girl who moved here from Cali. Blonde, tall, tan and beautiful. You know—a typical Blonde Clone Pretty Girl."

"Ok. Cool." And she went back to eating her pancakes—her fave.

"Mom? Mom, you ready? Zac?" I yell up the stairs.

"Coming, Gracie," I hear my mom answer.

"Me too, but hey, Gracie, fix me some food, sis? Please?" Zac calls.

I dish up pancakes for Mom and Zac. Pour generous glasses of milk, and smother all of their pancakes in Beth's homemade syrup she created.

Sundays are church days. We all go to the morning meetings. I enjoy it. Lifts my weary, teenage, angst spirit.

With breakfast conquered, we load ourselves into Zac's "on lend" BMW and drive off to church. The weather is really shaping up nicely. April in Texas is always up and down. Lots of rain. The humidity and heat begin creeping in. Temperatures start their uphill rise. Since spring break has officially started, I am looking forward to possibly sitting out on the patio after church today and soaking in some serious rays while reading my new *In Style*. I realize I need to make some plans with Zac, Mom, and Beth this week *and* with Clara, Justin, and maybe Brooke?

Later today, Zac, Beth and I are planning to play Boggle. It is a Sunday night tradition. Mom usually makes popcorn, then we all play for a few hours. It is usually a "family only" time. Sometimes no friends, girlfriends, etc., but not always. Even though it isn't quite the same without Dad, I'm glad Mom keeps up this family activity. We love the competition and camaraderie and that it's just our family.

"Zac! You are literally destroying us in Boggle tonight!"

He just laughs and throws some popcorn at my head.

"Hey! I just washed my hair today. Rude!" And throw some popcorn back at HIS head!

Beth wins twice. I win three times. Zac wins five times and Mom? One time, ha ha.

It's always fun, nonetheless, even if Zac wins all the games! Popcorn eaten, games won, laughs and great conversation amongst us, we then drag our tired selves off to bed.

I should mention that no matter what, Clara and I try to text each other each night. We've done it ever since we got our first phones for our b-days during our eighth grade year.

'How was your Sunday?'

'Chill u?'

'Same. Should we have movie nights all next week after work?'

'Great idea. Night.'

'Night.'

Though we have no school—due to spring break—Zac and I still have to work all week, as does Mom. Beth says she will be in and out with her friends all week, but I am hoping to make some good money this week at work, and to do some serious hanging out with Clara and Justin.

But! I don't think I can hang all week with Brooke, though. Not *all* week. I'm just not sure I can handle too much perfection being around me all the time. Just as I say these words in my brain about Brooke, I actually begin to have a tinge of guilt. Ugh. I shake THAT feeling off rapidly, so I can let it go and continue to get ready for bed.

"I will revisit this later, Fiona," I say matter-of-factly to my flamingo stuffie I have had since I was a little girl. I continue, "And, even though we all had a lot of fun together on Saturday, I am still very, very wary."

I fling Fiona over to the wall and crawl into my bed. I grab my journal.

'I adore Sundays! It's my favorite day for my family. Zac won most of the Boggle games, ha ha. Church was pleasant. A few new move-ins. Clara and her mom were there, too. Spring break this week! Work and movie binging all week!

I slam my journal shut, place it back on my side table, click off my light, and settle in for a good long read. I love to read before bed, so I pull out my Kindle and pick up where I left off. I'm finishing *Pride and Prejudice* by Jane Austen. Truly one of my faves.

CHAPTER SEVEN

ood morning, Spring Break! It is 10:15 am—time enough for me to lounge about and then get ready for work. I'll pack lunch and snacks for my long days like today. I work from twelve to eight pm today (Monday) and then, five hours Tuesday through Thursday. Then, all day Friday and Saturday.

Saturday night comes way more quickly than I hope! I crawl up the stairs. I am beat! I make it to my bathroom and stare at myself in the mirror. "Hey mirror! I look awful—ha ha—BUT! I did manage to make a ton of money, so that is good. Yay for me! I also did get to sit by our pool here and there and that was my other goal I wanted to accomplish. As for my social life, you ask?" You know I am speaking to an inanimate object—so no response—obvi. "Well, Justin ended up hanging with Brooke all week long, while Clara and I worked. But, every night, she and I watched so many fabulous chick flicks, and that was so worth it! Remind me to thank Justin, actually, for taking one for the team and totally keeping Clone Girl away from me all week!"

I wash my face, brush my teeth, and fall into bed without texting, journaling, nada... I am dead tired. No movies tonight either. I drift off in about three nanoseconds.

"Cock-a-doodle-doo! Cock-a-doodle-doo! Cock-a-doodle-doo!!"

Maybe, I need to get a new alarm clock! Sheesh.

"Argh… it cannot be Monday already, can it?" I whine to Fiona. Her cute head flops to the side. She agrees.

I drag myself out of my fabulous bed, make it (it's a hard and fast house rule—make your bed!) and groggily walk into my bathroom.

"Hello mirror," I greet my lovely mirror, squint my eyes, admire my slightly bronzed skin (I really DID get some sun this week) and begin the get-ready-for-school routine.

"How did Sunday come and go so quickly? Blah. Now I have to hang on until the end of school. Oh, man. Wish me luck, mirror!"

As I am applying my mascara, I continue to talk to my mirror.

"So, spring break was good—passed a little too quickly—oh no, I almost forgot, mirror, Brooke! She's in my first period and two other classes with me. Dang. It!"

I roll my eyes (you will come to see that this is my signature move) and finish getting ready and try NOT to overthink any of it!

I smell her before I even see her. She somehow spots me in the hallway just before we are entering ELAR in room 118.

"Oh, my gosh, hi, Gracie. Where were you all week? We had soooooo much fun. Justin came over and we swam. We went to the movies. Out to eat every day and shopping. Thank you for introducing me to Justin. He's so nice to me and does everything for me! Oh, but we totally missed you, really." She has a tiny pout on her perfect lips.

And I can obviously glean that she couldn't have cared less that I was with them or not. She's so shallow and devoid of actual kind feelings, it makes me nutso. Ew. I roll my eyes and turn away and walk into our room. I slightly grin at her and then I practically sprint to my desk. I deliberately pull out my book—*Pride and Prejudice*. I try to read it yearly. Anyways, I pick up on chapter five as I hear the other students clamber into the room and plunk down into their chairs.

English begins and Brooke has her own group that she's been assigned to, thankfully, so I'm spared any more interaction with her for now. But though we don't interact, thoughts start to niggle in my brain. Thoughts like: SO MUCH for my plan to NOT have Blondie

Girl interfere in my social life. Well, I guess it was just Justin she stole, and in reality I wouldn't have had any time to actually hang, since I had worked too much to be able to do anything with, so to be fair, this was understandable? Plus, I *did* still owe $200 for Brooke's car repair. I *can* say that I appreciated the extra work, and that moolah will cover that cost.

"I need to focus!" I tell myself, suddenly. We've got three desks pulled together for my group. We're studying poetry and comparing a few poems. While in my daze of rando thoughts, I manage to bend down at the same time someone walks between the chairs. He trips over my backpack, and he ends up kicking my hand.

"Owwwww!" I yelp.

"Oh, my gosh, I'm so sorry! Did I hurt you?"

"I'm okay. Just stings a bit. It's cool. Are you okay?"

It's at this time that I look up a bit to see who tripped over my backpack and who kicked my hand. His voice didn't sound familiar. And as I look up at him, I am sure my face shows the shock as I see this boy's amazing face.

He smiles at me with perfect white teeth and looks at me with a pair of the most fabulous ice-blue eyes I've ever seen. I turn twelve shades of red and quickly spin around. Brooke—being the nosy person she is—ends up coming over to us all, steps over my backpack with amazing grace, and sticks out her hand to him.

"Hi. I'm Brooke... and, wait, Jake? For real? What are you doing *here*? Um, Gracie, this is Jake. We knew each other in Cali."

But, and I notice this immediately, he doesn't take her perfectly manicured hand with the

Barbie pink polish on them. Instead, he just says, "Hi. I'm Jake. Nice to meet you, Gracie. Brooke, good to see you."

I watch as Brooke sort of winces and smiles weirdly and goes back to her desk and group.

I turn back toward Jake just in time to see him smile again, and I actually feel faint.

"Is this seat taken?" he asks politely.

He's gesturing to the desk that's across from me. I can't speak one word, so Jake says, "Thanks." Sitting where he is makes him part of MY group. He scoots his desk closer to us all and asks what we're studying.

"Poetry?" I say quietly. I show Jake the two poems, and we continue our discussion.

My brain finally catches up with what's just happened around me. THIS JUST IN: my brief encounter with this new, hot guy is already over! You know it is Gracie! There's no WAY with Jake *already* knowing Blondie from California that I even have half of a chance in you know what with him. Heck no. No way. BUT, I am remembering that I also realize that Jake sort of snuffed Brooke. Right? Did I sense that? Despite my "I've got no chance," thinking, I still end up daydreaming about Jake and his eyes and gentle smile.

I feel like I have been in a real-life comatose state all day. Like I'm just shuffling from class to class all day long! Sheesh. Get a grip!

The first period bell rings. I sprint out into the hall and hide in the steady flow of students. I think I hear Brooke call out to me, but I ignore it and get to second period. Choir is third period, and as mentioned before, I sit by Clara—and Brooke sits on the other side—so no convo. Phew. I shuffle through my day. Class. Bell. Class. Bell. Then, finally the sixth period rings. Hallelujah! Almost done with my day.

"What the heck is wrong with me?" I speak to myself, well, actually to the inside of my locker, while I grab my Latin book, just before my last period, which is Latin. All I can think of right now is *WHERE IS MY BATHROOM MIRROR* for this convo? Boy, do I need it! I continue to talk to my locker.

'It's not like I even saw Jake at all today, other than after English class, so what is the big deal? Why am I using any amount of my brain capacity to allow myself to think about Jake? What in the world is wrong with me? Good grief. It's me! Hello! Gracie! The mellow one. The one who doesn't really care about any of this stuff.'

I think to myself that I am very glad that I haven't seen Jake again since this morning, 'cause I knew for a fact that I won't be able to even carry on a normal conversation with him! Par Example: this morning when I said nothing and simply gawked. Tongue-tieditis. Frozenitis. Whatever it is, it is ridiculous and a waste of my time. Good grief!" I slam my locker and turn to go toward Latin class and bolt down the hallway to B-134. While walking, I quickly send off a text to Clara.

'New hot guy in my first period.'

'Oh yeah, Jake, right? He's in one of my classes, too. Really nice guy.'

I put my phone into my back pocket and waltz into my Latin classroom and look to my left as I stride to my table, and who do I see?

I see HIM. JAKE—there in *my* Latin class talking to the teacher.

"WHAT IS HE DOING in this class?" Mind you, this a very small class, like there are only eight people total, well, now nine including Jake. I briefly glance at Jake's back—he is turned around talking to the two boys on the table behind him.

I, in turn, scurry in like a scared mouse, and sit down rapidly in my chair—WHICH I NEED TO BE CLEAR: my seat is next to HIM. I slide into my chair and immediately I look down at my desk. I legit keep my head down. Actually, I find a pattern in the desk and follow it like I'm doing a maze with my eyeballs.

This keeps me occupied for a nanosecond, and then without being able to control my eyeballs, I tear my eyes away from the twenty pencil holes I just counted ten times and take a chance to look over at Jake, only to find that he's looking at me and his eyes lock on mine. Holy cannoli.

'Uh oh.' My brain shoots me a warning sign.

He smiles at me. I give some sort of weird smile and turn away abruptly.

"It's Gracie, right?"

I turn to face him.

"Um, yes?"

"Yes? or yes." He laughs.

"Yes." I swallow hard.

He smiles at me. I melt like a popsicle in the Texas heat. His smile is contagious. And his eyes are *so* blue.

I faintly hear Mr. Davis welcome us, and then suddenly he turns his attention to me.

"Oh, excellent, Gracie, this gentleman right next to you is Jake. He needs some help catching up in Latin, and I immediately thought of you, since you are the top Latin 3 student. Would you mind helping him?"

"Uh, uh, um, sure?" Again my intonation rises.

"Sure? or sure."

"Sure." I smile and put my head down again. I want to be magic right now and open a hole in the ground and crawl down into it. Instead, I open our interactive Latin notebook and try to focus on the words.

I can feel a vibration next to me as Jake laughs.

Argh. LET THIS DAY BE OVER!

I can barely concentrate for the entire period. I take turns looking at my book, then to my teacher, and periodically stealing looks at Jake. I'm staring at the clock on the wall—the bell is about to ring—when I hear Jake say some words to me. At least, I think they're real words. Apparently, I have returned to my zombie-comatose state without even knowing it.

"So, Gracie," Jake says, piercing me through like a dagger with his amazing blue eyes. They are like little blue swimming pools, and I want to dive right in….

"So, I just came from California. Can you tell me what Texas is like?"

"Hot?"

"Is that a question or a statement?" Jake gives me a little smile while chuckling at me.

I giggle to myself.

"Hot. Entertaining. A Mecca of culture and fun."

"Sounds nice. Sounds like a place I would like. So, when do you want to get together and study?"

Was he still talking to me? He was looking at me, and his mouth was moving. I snap out of my crazed state in order to answer.

"Um, tonight?"

He laughs.

"Ha, ha. Okay. Tonight is good for me. Let me give you my cell number." I watch as he grabs my phone and types in his number, in utter disbelief.

"Just text me your address. I'm going to try out for the track team after school, even though it's a little late in the year, but my dad talked to the coach and told him I've already been involved in track in my old school, so it should work out okay. So how about 7:30 pm?"

"Sure."

Sure? That's all that comes out of my mouth? Sure? Good grief.

The bell rings. Jake grabs his stuff, turns to me and says, "Bye, Gracie. See you tonight. Don't forget to text me your address!" And he is out the door before I can utter yet another one-word response.

I grab my stuff, too, and haul outta class. No work today, but projects, so I've got to get home. Home... home! All I can think of is that hottie Jake is coming to MY home tonight.

MY HOME.

CHAPTER EIGHT

I find Old Blue, unlock it, and jump inside. Boy, is it HOT. I put the air conditioning on first thing, then open the two front windows. It's a Texas thing: hot air out, cold air replaces it. It's finally feeling cooler, so I back out and start for my house, and there waiting is Blondie.

Crappity crap, I think! I forget every day that I have to take her to and from school until her precious Mustang is fixed. This task alone could ruin even a pretty good high school day for me. I unlock the doors, and she glides in and without fail, she starts her incessant babbling the minute she gets in.

"Hi, Gracie. Did you see Jake at all throughout the day? He's in like three of my other classes. Oh, he is so dreamy. Did you see his eyes? Hear his voice? See his rippling muscles?"

"Uh, who?"

"You know, that guy you ran into this morning in English? Jake? He's in AP World History, Geometry, and Health with me. I waved him over each time in class to sit by me. But, ha ha, he must not have seen me."

I decided to be mean. I just couldn't help it.

"Wait, what are you talking about? What about Justin? You aren't going to break his heart, are you? He's been my friend for a long time."

"What are *you* talking about? Pfff—he and I are just friends. Please. It's Jake I want." And I swear I see an evil glint in her eyes. You know, like in the movies. Freaky.

I pull up to her house. Happy to be rid of this human who is making my life crazy.

Happily, I roast Old Blue right out of her precious neighborhood. I can see her lips moving but hear none of her words since my truck is so loud. I look in my rear-view mirror just as she waves her perfectly manicured hand. I gave her a half-hearted wave and blaze down the street.

The entire time, my mind is replaying all of the conversations I had with Jake in first and seventh period. And then my mind turns to what Brooke just said to me about Justin. And then I just feel anger, so much anger, because I cannot have Justin broken again. And I cannot handle a repeat of freshman year, nor can I handle this stupid girl who is actually so mean and so selfish!

I make it home, just in time to see Beth get dropped off from one of her friends' moms. The moms all rotate each week for pickup and drop off. I run upstairs and fling my stuff onto my bed, then run back downstairs to the kitchen. Once I've had something to eat, I think to myself, I text Clara.

'Jake is in my Latin class and is coming over for help to MY HOUSE tonight.'

'Cool! Have fun.'

Cool have fun? What the actual? Not cool! Not cool AT ALL! Terrifying is what it is….

The rest of the afternoon is a wash, because there is just a continuous stream of thoughts in my mind. It is a regular old ping pong match between reality and my dreams. The burning question that keeps surfacing is this: Why is Jake being so nice to the likes of me when Blondie is in the picture?

It has to be a ruse. I mean, I'm sort of a middle-ground-type girl. I think I am sort of pretty, well, maybe cute is more like it, and I def have brains. This is the part I like most about myself. I cultivate intelligence. I seek after it in fact. I read and read and study and I love to learn. Love. It.

If I am to describe my looks, I can describe me as this: I have a dark complexion with medium length-layered hair. I stand at a medium height, I am relatively thin, but not like a true Betty, really.

In my dazed state, I do manage to text Jake and give him my address.

'My address is 3204 Ashton Way.'

'Cool. See you later on.'

Then, doubt and self-realization set in, and I convince myself that he is definitely not going to follow through with the study session. After all, he is ridiculously good-looking and apparently athletic, as I had felt earlier when he hit me with his buff arm and backpack. And that combo equaled the "not into my mousey-type" category. He is definitely a match for the Blonde Clone Girl.

Not me.

Before I know it, it's already 7:15 pm. Zac and Beth are both gone, and Mom is in her study. No texts from Jake. Just as I had figured. Probably hanging with Blondie Clone. Whatever.

Suddenly, the text message alert flashes. It's Brooke.

"Kill me now," I say to my phone.

"What the?"

Her text says:

'Jake and I on the way to you. Met Jake at track.'

And she continues for an entire paragraph.

Apparently, Blondie went to go and watch Jake. Her mom dropped her off after she'd got home (so why she couldn't pick up Brooke is beyond me). They get to talking after and he finds out that she and I know each other and that she knows where I live and she actually needs help with English, so could she come too? AND voila!

WOAH, woah, woah... All of a sudden, Brooke and I are now FRIENDS? Oh please, I loathe the girl! Okay, maybe not a full on loathe, but close. Oh, but wait, there's more... now this means Jake and Brooke will be an item in about a Peloponnesian minute.

"Oh, this is gonna be a *great* evening," I yell at my cell!

Speaking to inanimate objects is something I do a lot, I realize.

I text her back.

'Sounds good.'

Short and sweet. But it is NOT good, and boy, it is anything *but* sweet. In fact, I am seething. I run upstairs and try to make myself look somewhat decent.

"Here it goes again! Beautiful girl gets beautiful guy," I mutter grumpily to my mirror as I attempt to make my hair look less out of control.

I collect myself, take a last minute once-over check, and slump down the stairs. I set up my Latin and ELAR books and my coordinating notebooks, all on the dining room table. Then I wait. And while I wait, I fume.

I truly needed to let this go. I am never going to win at this game. Ever.

Five minutes later, I hear a car motor. Doors bang open and shut. Skittering at my door. Giggly laughter. Ugh. Then the knock comes.

"Let the fun begin!" I retort to myself angrily. I take a deep breath and then plaster on a Cheshire-cat-like smile and open the door.

"Hey guys, come on in!" And then as if I've just been hit by a brick, I have a lightbulb idea pop into my brain once I see Jake's ice blue eyes.

You know what? I can and will play this little game with Brooke, and I too can lay on the sugary sweetness very, very thick. Brooke can't have everything *and* be perfect, too.

"Let's come into the dining room. Better lighting for studying." I laugh and speak simultaneously, sounding like a sick hyena.

Jake and Brooke sit down. Brooke scoots her chair toward Jake and sits as close as possible. Boy! She is laying on her flirtatiousness pretty thick.

Flirting just does not come naturally for me. I have seen this act already with Justin and about every boy she comes in contact with at school, or anywhere, for that matter. Same with Katy from Freshman year. And as Katy didn't disappoint me in my assumptions of her, neither is Brooke. She is just as I suspect her to be: a perfect, plastic, too pretty, too sweet, flirtatious, boy-magnet Blondie Clone. Oh, and apparently smart since she is in AP World History with Jake.

What is up with *that*? If she's in AP World History, then she can't be that lost in English.

But then it hits me—she really doesn't need my help in English at all, and this is obviously a ploy to hang with Jake.

Grrrrr.

"You guys need some water? Snacks? Great! I'll be right back." I don't wait for a response. I just move quickly into the kitchen. Breathing deeply, I console myself.

'Okay. Get the water. Pop some popcorn. Go back in. You can do it." I take in the water while the popcorn pops in the microwave, and then grab it out as soon as the chime dings.

"Well, we better get started Jake, since I have other homework to do..." My voice trails off.

Okay, I do not understand how people can think straight when being looked at by someone as beautiful as Jake and with those eyes that melt my heart every time.

I need to get a grip! It's not like I've never been around boys before, good gracious! I've even liked other boys before. What is my deal?!

"Great. I really appreciate you taking the time to help me, Gracie. I know you work and go to school, so your time is valuable. So, thanks."

I just look at him, attempting to keep the jaw-dropping motion about to happen, to NOT happen. Beautiful AND nice? Holy.

Two hours whiz by, then Jake and Brooke are gone. It had gone okay. Brooke didn't have a Latin clue, so I was able to be triumphant in that area. Instead, she just ogled her eyes at Jake, batting her eyelashes and saying ridiculous things all night long.

She should know guys already swoon over her because of her looks, because, let's be real, she is so beautiful. So why is she trying so hard?

I crawl up to bed. I am exhausted. All that trying hard to *not* be myself took wayyyyyy too much energy, and I ended up dropping the whole charade once I started helping Jake with Latin. I am glad I finally gave up and went back to being plain, old, boring, sarcastic me.

Jake didn't seem to mind. Of course, I never even helped Brooke with any English, which is just as I suspected would happen.

"Oh well. Tomorrow is the end of the week—Friday," I tell Fiona, and relief washes over me knowing it is soon to be the weekend. "I have to work the Friday night shift and have an early Saturday shift, so my socializing is quite limited this weekend—oh, wait. It already is limited to my family, my work, and maybe Justin and Clara, ha ha!"

This is what I have been telling Fiona. I stumble through my night routine: pick an outfit. Wash my face. Brush my teeth. Brush my hair. I still have to finish an English assignment, so I put on my Lofi Nuaic list and get 'er done! I also have a little math, and I still have some history.

Two hours later, with my backpack packed and assignments done, I happily climb into my bed. "Ahhh," I whisper to myself. "This is my happy place." Kindle in hand, I turn out my light and deep dive into *Pride and Prejudice*. Three more chapters left....

CHAPTER NINE

'*N*ight was actually good with Jake, oh, and Brooke came, too.' I text Clara.

'Oh good! So glad. C U tomorrow.'

I can never be fully honest with Clara. Sigh. Makes me a little crazy. She's just a good person through and through and literally loves and accepts everyone. I def need to be way more like her, but I am super protective of Justin and my SOUL, sooooo I am wary. Very, very wary!!

So what I wanted to say was this: BROOKE IS SO MUCH TO DEAL WITH. SHE IS FLIRTY. SHE IS OVERWHELMING. SHE TRIES WAY TOO HARD WITH JAKE. But, I end up writing this into my "therapy journal." Good thing, otherwise these feelings would fester and build up until I have an emotional volcanic eruption inside of me!

By the time I finish washing my face, I am very tired—more emotionally weary than physically—and as I am brushing my teeth, I hear doors closing and know that Zac, Beth, and Mom are already getting ready for bed.

Although I'm still feeling bugged at Brooke and how this evening tried, yet failed to turn into the Brooke show, I do a few sun salutations and breathe out the anger so I can sleep. And, I remind myself, luckily for me, Brooke has zero knowledge of Latin, and I am actually stellar at it, so that is a win for me.

"Why?" I think stubbornly to myself. "Why do I care so much this time about this Brooke and Jake situation?"

My brain doesn't answer. Instead, I realize I am living a telenovela in real life and I already am NOT looking forward to first period tomorrow, since Brooke is in there and will start her excessive babbling all about Jake.

I plunk into bed, feeling a bit sorry for myself or feeling bugged and for caring. I grab my woobie and Fiona and my Kindle. Time to read away my emotions and get some rest! It's a whole new day tomorrow of playing emotional pickle ball with Brooke, so I need to be ready!

I thought Jake wasn't staying in first period—he had mentioned that—but low and behold, he is there looking ridiculously good. He is wearing a baby pink NIKE shirt that makes his eyes pop even more, if that is possible.

I move to my seat quietly and slide in, when who comes floating in just as I seat myself? Yep. BLONDIE. I choose to pull out my Kindle (I pack it with me every day—you never know when a time to read can occur, so I like to be prepared!) then I will be spared having to watch Brooke flirt with Jake immediately upon her arrival. Bless up!

While I am trying very hard to concentrate on my reading, I suddenly realize that all my dreams last night were of Brooke! I remember Brooke looking very much like Godzilla, and she was squashing me and was grabbing Jake in her hands to have forever. It was slightly disturbing, to say the least.

"Back to your book, Gracie," I prod my own self. "Better to block it all out."

I have resolved to do this every morning or anytime dumb thoughts creep into my brain, when I see what Brooke is wearing as she floats into her seat. "Man!" I say under my breath, "How is she looking better than ever?" She is pretty in pink from head to toe—a pink tight belly shirt, a short denim pink striped miniskirt, and the cutest pink wedges I've ever seen!

I watch as she literally lowers herself meticulously into the chair in front of me, and immediately says "hi" to Jake, and starts chatting his ears off, I swear!

'Welp! There go all of my chances to even have a convo with Jake. I mean, who am I kidding? As if I HAVE any chance at all, so why do I keep holding onto a string of hope? Why was I holding out with some semblance of desire to be noticed by Jake?'

This is the sermon I'm telling myself. And, I am, of course, dressed in my typical attire—jeans, a T-shirt, and flat sandals. My hair is pulled back into a simple ponytail, a no-nonsense hairstyle. I snort under my breath and say to no one in particular, "I was under the impression that attending school is to become educated, not to pretend that a photo shoot is going to bust out at any minute." I roll my eyes and bury my head into my Kindle again.

"Morning, Gracie. Isn't it just a fantabulous day?" Brooke oozes these words out and into the air around me, not waiting for my response apparently, and whips her fresh-scented hair across the pages of my book—again. Then, as if one hair-whip across a page isn't enough, there it is again. "Whipppppp!" And her hair is always so fragrant like every time!

She continues to babble to Jake and turns every so often toward me, too, but always like I am an afterthought.

"So, do you like my new outfit? My dad totally got it in Italy on his business trip. I love it! Brings out my blue eyes and my blond hair, n'est pas? That's French for doesn't it!"

And the hair whips across my Kindle AGAIN, only this time it lingers there and covers my entire book.

"Seriously?" I say under my breath as I move her dang hair out of the way. My brain can't comprehend what's happening. "Sure. Nice outfit," I retort with as much evident sarcasm as I can without being too cruel.

Oh! As I move her perfect Clone Doll hair out of the way, I

suddenly register the fact that her face is flawless. Like FLAWLESS. I moan and close my eyes and take four deep breaths.

Despite however much covering-up I do, I still have tiny freckles on both of my cheeks. I gave up trying some time ago and just stick to cover-up and mascara and some lip gloss. Not like Clone Girl and half the female population at my school who wear pounds of make-up. Ew. How do they even stand it? How do the guys STAND it? Yuck.

I grab my Kindle and hide behind it. I've been reading and rereading the same paragraph a billion times. I focus and plow through my next chapter.

"Hey Grace, What's up? Thanks again for your help last night."

I am shaken out of my reverie as I hear Jake talking. Talking to ME. Not Brooke.

"Hey Jake. Yeah, no problemo!"

Okay, like what, do I speak Spanish now?

Jake laughs. I give him a sheepish grin and thankfully for me, Mr. McFadden calls us to order and begins class. Today's discussion is the beginning of our novel study of *Frankenstein* by Mary Shelly. I've never read this book, so I am looking forward to reading it and discussing it.

Mid-way through class, Mr. McFadden puts us in groups of four. Of course, I have Brooke in my group, and this super-smart girl named Rachel, but we do get Jake, so that's cool.

As we are pulling our desks together to discuss the first three chapters, Brooke scoots herself right up as close to Jake as possible. Rachel scoots by me and we make some sort of misshapen square. Our discussion is to be about human nature and the character of Dr. Frankenstein.

We have a pretty decent discussion, write down our comments, and then try to choose a spokesperson. Jake leads out in that decision, and then he suggests me! I don't know why the heck he does this, but I do happen to see a look on Brooke's face that she is *not* happy with Jake picking me.

Not gonna lie, I have a twinge of contentment wash over me. Ha.

Mr. McFadden comes around the room to check in with all the groups and to have the group spokespersons take turns sharing. Before I know it, he's standing by our group and right by me. I start to feel heat rush up into my cheeks as if they are on fire. My palms even feel sweaty. CRAP.

I usually don't care about anyone around me. I just do my thing and boom—I'm done. Now, with Jake peering into my soul and Brooke leering at me, I am actually terrified I will come off like a total idiot. I try to follow what we have discussed and share that info.

We came up with one simple point: Intelligent people are fascinating. Their ideas can be life-changing and so useful and helpful, except when the intelligence goes a bit overboard—like with Dr. Frankenstein. Thoughts of creating a creature are really creepy and very frowned upon.

Phew! I manage not to slaughter our discussion thoughts and finish, feeling very relieved. The bell rings, and I run like prey from its enemy. I am both entranced and scared to death of Jake—his beauty, his kindness, and that he's actually been talking to me!

Suddenly, someone grabs my hand as I am whisking myself out of the classroom. The hand is warm, slightly calloused and strong. I keep holding it until I can turn to see its owner.

No. Way.

It's Jake's hand.

"Hey, where are you going in such a rush? Nice job on sharing our group's thoughts."

"Yeah, um, thanks. Gotta get to the next period." I sort of laugh-talk these words. I'm such a dork.

"Whoa, okay, well, me too, ha ha—but, can I ask you something?"

"Uh, sure?"

"Do you have plans for Saturday?"

"Ummm, well—work, I work until three pm. Sorry." My words sound sad and clipped.

"Ok, cool. Wanna go get a bite to eat after?"

"Wait. For real? With me?"

"Yes, you. Well, do 'ya?"

"Okay, sure. I guess. Um, but what about Brooke? Won't she be mad?"

"Brooke? Mad? Why would she be mad?"

"Oh, well, I thought you two are like going out. She's always hanging on you or with you, so I just assumed—"

"No. We aren't," he says this very abruptly and cuts me off. "So, is that a yes?"

"Okay, yeah, sure." I smile and look at him long enough to soak in his warm smile and his kind eyes.

"How about around five o'clock? I have some chores and stuff to do around my house. We can talk about more details later when I see you in Latin, today, okay?" he suggests.

"Okay, sure!"

"See 'ya, Gracie...."

"Bye." I stand stalk still in the hallway as the hordes of high school kids swarm around me. What just happened? DO I HAVE A DATE? ME?"

And with those words, he is gone and became immediately swallowed in a sea of high-schoolers all in a mad dash down a too-crowded hallway.

I stare down the hallway after him like a baby doe with huge, sappy eyes.

'Alright, what just happened? Was I just asked out by Jake to go and eat tomorrow night? And when I mentioned Brooke, did Jake act weird about that question, or was that just me hoping?' I whisper to myself as I cruise to my next class, but of course I am in a daze again and I run right into some guy and all my books fell to the floor.

He didn't even care. Just walked off. Jerk. I pick them up and continue to move in this slight daze throughout the rest of the day until the last period—Latin—when I suddenly remember I would see Jake, since he is in class with me.

I text Clara quickly.

'Jake asked me to go out with him Saturday. I am officially freaking out.'

'Ahh that's so great! What are you going to wear?'

'I have zero idea. I'll send a few pics later of some outfit choices.'

'Cool-bye!'

I walk into the classroom and plunk my books down. It has been an emotional and very long week for me! I am not good at playing these guy-girl games at all.

I end up arriving a little early to Latin, since in my previous class, which is Science, we had a sub, and she let us out five minutes early. I pull out my Latin text and my notebook and start flipping through the pages to find our assignment to work on for the day. Next week we have a major test, so it is major review time. All of the Latin roots.

Thankfully, Latin comes pretty easily to me. I pull out my index cards, my markers, and busy myself by continuing to write all the roots and their meanings down.

BAM! I about jump out of my skin! Holy! I look up and there he is —Jake.

"Oh, ha ha, sorry! I didn't mean to scare you, Gracie!"

"Oh, no, I'm good, ha ha, really. I was just concentrating on making flashcards for the test next week."

"Nice. You really like to study and read, don't ya? Me too."

"I do… and you do, too?"

It is at this point that I freeze mid-sentence because all I can see is Jake's blue eyes—perfectly clear blue like a picture of tropical waters. Amazing. I just want to dive in, and slowly drown into those eyes…

"Uh, Gracie? You okay?" Jake is smiling and I think giggling. His teeth are beautiful. His lips… oh, my. Did he know I am staring straight into HIS EYES? I finally snap out of it. Finally!

"Yeah, so good, and you?"

"Great. I think I'm gonna like this school." He laughs. "So, the test is next Wednesday. Are you up for a study group together on Tuesday night? I have track until six pm then I am free."

"I will check my work schedule. My managers are cool about switching when I have exams."

"Cool."

And then he turns to his book and for the rest of the period, we make light conversation and discuss Latin roots.

It's the best. *He* is the best. I haven't come across a guy who I actually am starting to like, who isn't just a friend, and so nice, too. I just know something will def go wrong, and that I am living in a real-life dream and I'd wake up and get slapped by reality at any moment!

Argh. My thoughts annoy me soooo much. If only I was more confident in myself... if only!

But for now, I am in heaven....

CHAPTER TEN

So, you know how most people actually have something to look forward to on the weekends? Well, I usually don't. Just work, family, homework and school. But now, I have an actual date tomorrow night.

I am so antsy. I am so nervous. I am so excited. It's like a trifecta of swirling emotions. I can hardly keep up.

Thankfully, Friday night comes and goes quickly. I am exhausted, so I am now watching a chick-flick and eating cookie dough straight from the container, when Beth mosies in and actually has some time to hang with me.

"Oh my! My own sister-here-with me! How's life Gracie?"

"Good. Busy. Going on a date tomorrow."

"Woah. What? You *never* go on "date-dates.""

"I know."

"So, what's his name?"

"Jake."

"Jake?"

"Yeah. Jake. I don't even know his last name. He's just Jake. Blue eyes. White teeth. So nice. Smart. And he asked *me* out."

"Gracie, please! You're so pretty and smart and fun! You have got to stop this nonsense."

"Ha, thanks Beth. You're sweet, but you know you have to say those things 'cause you're my sister."

"Gee, Gracie, come on now. No, I really don't. I mean it. You're smart, pretty, kind—you're a catch!"

"Okay, whatever, little sis. Let's talk about you. How was your week?"

"Busy. Busy, and more busy. I did make it to round three of the spelling bee, though! I now have one week to prepare for the last and final round. I'm actually very, very nervous."

"Oh, my gosh! I am so proud of you. I know you can win this, Beth. You're such a smart girl and you put in the work to be successful!"

"I guess… it's sooooo stressful though. Lots of studying to do, 'ya know?"

"You're so disciplined, and that is such a great trait that you have!"

"Yeah, I guess. Um, want some popcorn?"

"Sure, and I'll grab some apple juice for us both."

Beth and I watch two movies—*Bride Wars* and *Bridesmaids*—and laugh and laugh until we can laugh no more. Man, I love this sister of mine.

And then it's Saturday.

I wake up early. Why? 'Cause I'm already nervous! I shower, dress quickly, and haul off to work.

We open at 10:30 am on Saturdays, since we are closed on Sundays, so lots of people will come in today and get pizzas to refrigerate for Sunday.

We have a new pizza topping we are debuting today. It's called Leaning Tower of Pisa, a meat and cheese lovers delight.

Then, before I can even say mamma mia, it's three pm. I clock out and literally peel out in Old Blue and race home to get in another shower and then try and pull together some sort of cute outfit to make myself look presentable. I have a few options I planned out and took some pics of last night and sent them to Clara.

I pull around my favorite corner where I can see our cute yellow house with the crepe myrtles in the front yard. They are starting to wake with the spring air and are nearly ready to blossom in full force–pink and white. Lovely.

Then I see it. The red Mustang. Shiny, new, *and* in my driveway. I park on the street and get out. Brooke. And she is still in her car. As I walk by, she jumps out and almost attacks me as I near her car.

"So, hey Gracie, what are you doing right now?"

"Um, hey Brooke, hey, yeah, well, I'm gonna take a shower and eat."

"What are you doing *after* that, 'cause I came over to see if you want to hang with Clara, Justin, and me. We're all going to the movies and to eat. I texted Jake, but he said he couldn't hang 'cause he already had plans. Can you believe that? He said he had other plans. No one ever, ever turns me down. As if! Grrrr. I am soooo mad."

"Huh. Well, I sure wish I could join y'all, but I have to do some studying and chores around here, too. So, uh, see 'ya."

I walk briskly past her and to my front door, and do not allow myself to turn around, but just open and shut my front door as quickly as possible. I skip stairs to get to my room quickly. I slink down and crawl on my floor to be able to look out of my bedroom window.

I peek over the windowsill and watch as Brooke slams her door shut. I can see her mad face through her front window. She grinds her gears and jams her car in reverse, and then noisily peels out of my driveway.

"I think she's really ticked." I chuckle to myself. I continue to giggle as I lay out a few of my outfit choices and take a shower. And all I can think of is WHAT IS happening? Has the universe gone all topsy turvy? Blondie mad at ME? Plain old, Gracie? How ironic. I smile wryly at myself in my favorite mirror.

"Such a turn of events for this girl. I NEVER have this stuff happen to me. Like NEVER."

I try on five different outfits trying to get myself ready. I finally just put on one of the new skirts I purchased a few weeks ago. Yellow based with small daisies on it. The shirt is a simple V-neck in a lighter yellow. I give myself the once over and strap on my new sandals.

"All ready to go with thirty minutes to spare!" I tell my mirror.

He's such a good listener. I wink at myself and start to pace back and forth across my room. I'm feeling a little queasy with nervousness. Going out with guys isn't something I've done very much. That's for sure. I decide to write in my journal. Maybe this will help me chill out.

"Saturday—I'm waiting to get picked up to go out with Jake, who is seriously hot and nice and kind all wrapped in one package! I'm nervous. I'm excited. I'm a little terrified if I'm being totally honest…."

I write a few more lines, then after about fifteen minutes, I saunter down the stairs. I actually feel like I look nice, and I feel happy too. Usually I'm not up or down, just somewhere in the middle. I'm liking these happy and more confident feelings. Much better than feeling like I'm a broken person.

I enter the kitchen—see my mom, Zac, and Beth. I have been in such a frenzy last week with work, the Brooke-Jake issue, and now this date. I feel like I haven't seen these beautiful people touched base all week!

"Wow! You look amazing Grace, really!"

"Thanks, Mom."

"Are you going somewhere, my dear?"

"Well, yes. It just so happens I'm going out with this new boy named Jake tonight. And before you all ask, yes, he is beautiful. Which has me feeling befuddled as to why he's going out with me tonight. But nonetheless he asked me out yesterday at school in Latin class and *not* Brooke and I am a nervous wreck!!"

They all three pause what they're doing and look at me with the craziest puzzled faces. Then they break into laughter. I mean, really guffawing and all.

"You guys!" I wine "I'm seriously nervous!"

"Sweetie, could you please give yourself a little more credit? I do not make ugly children."

"And this is coming from my beautiful mother. Yeah, you are my mother and my siblings. That doesn't count. Mom, you're my mom. You have to say this—"

"I don't have to, and I'm perfectly serious. You are beautiful, inside and out." She gives a little sigh as she said these words.

"Yeah, sis, go a little easy on yourself. Who is this kid anyway? Do I need to check him out?" Zac raises his eyebrows and flexes a bit.

"Okay, no, down boy, and he is actually really, really nice."

The glazed look has returned to my eyes unbeknownst to me, and I stop speaking mid-sentence.

"Gracie?" Beth brings me out of my trance.

"Okay, um, yeah, so listen everyone, when Jake gets here, everyone is to be calm and not ask him a million questions. Please! It's just one date, and it's not like we're dating or anything. I think we are going out to eat, that's all I know. You okay with that, Mom?"

"Yes, dear, but I do want Zac to meet him. You know, since your dad's been gone and all, it's good to have your older brother to fill in some of the "dad" roles in some cases...."

Poor mom. Her voice always trails off when she speaks of Dad.

"Of course, Mom. Wouldn't have it any other way."

Ding-dong-dong!

"That's the doorbell. It must be Jake...." I nearly jump out of my chair, knocking it to the floor.

"Nervous much, sis?" Zac can't help but laugh at me.

I am a wreck! Good grief. Breathe....

"Okay, okay," I whisper, giving a, "don't say it" expression, but with a smile.

Zac leaps to the door to answer it.

"Hey. Jake, is it? Come on in and meet the family." Zac gives a devious older brother smile. "This is our mother, Kathy, I'm Gracie's older brother, Zac, and this is Beth, our little sister."

"Nice to meet you all. Pleasure. Um, so I am going to take us to eat at that new Hideaway pizza place around the corner. And maybe go to a bookstore. Then I thought we would take a walk around since the weather is decent today, plus I'm new to Texas."

"Sounds lovely. Gracie was just telling all of us that y'all just moved here? How are you liking Texas?"

"I love it already. Both my parents grew up in Cali, so warmer weather is what they love. My sister, Meg, and I are acclimating just fine."

"Wait, Meg Kennethson? She's in my grade at Thomas Middle." This is Beth who just piped up.

"That's her. Do you know each other, uh, Beth, is it?"

"Yeah, she's great. I was totally going to ask my mom if I could have her over sometime soon."

"Cool." He smiles when he says this and looks—Right. At. Me.

Oh, I love when he smiles at me.

"Jake, here is my cell number and our home if you need us for anything. Have fun."

"Thanks, Zac," I glare at him, but with a teasing smile.

"See 'ya Mom! Zac! Beth!"

"Bye, have fun! Oh, what time will you be home you guys?"

"About 11:00 pm. Will that be okay, Mrs. Miller?"

"Oh, goodness, please call me Ms. Kathy, that's what my readers call me," she gave a goofy smile and actually blushed a little.

Jake opens the front door for me, gestures for me to go ahead, and then softly closes the door behind us. He opens my side of his car—a Jeep in a deep midnight blue—and I step up and in.

I look up to catch a little smile as he closes me in and our eyes meet. Briefly. I watch him walk around to his side. I follow his every move until he's in the car, buckles and starts the engine. The night is cool, so he has no top on the Jeep.

#dreamsdocometrue.

"Sweet car, Jake. Seriously cool."

"Thanks, Gracie. Bought it myself just a few months ago. I've had my eye on this Jeep for a long, long time."

"Impressive." We pull out and I catch a glimpse of my family as they stand and are peeking from behind the front door side drapes, on the long, narrow windows flanking the door.

Honestly. You'd think it is my first date.

Oh my gosh! It IS my first, real date! L-O-S-E-R that I am....

"Your family is so nice. But I didn't see your dad around. Working late, or is he out of town?"

"Um, he passed away almost three years ago now, so that's why Zac was extra-parental. He's taken on the "dad-role" pretty well."

Jake's facial expression droops and his eyes frown.

"Oh, Gracie, I am soooo sorry. I had no idea." He sort of whispered this.

"Of course you didn't. How could you? It's not like I told you." I grinned girlishly.

"Yeah, right. Okay. Anyway, I truly am sorry." He turns his head away from me and stares at the road ahead.

CHAPTER ELEVEN

We sit in silence for a minute or two. I don't want to have him feel badly over my dad, and as I am about to say something, he starts talking.

"So, uh, that's cool my sister knows your sister. Making friends has been a bit difficult for her with this move."

"This move?" I ask this with evident surprise in my voice.

"My dad's business has taken us all over. I hope this will be our last move since I am a junior. Staying put would be good."

"Wow, that's crazy you've moved so much! I've been here my whole life, actually, but I've always wondered what it would be like to move around. Do you like it or hate it?"

"Some places I've liked better than other places. I like Texas already and a lot quicker than other places. But maybe I like the people here, uh, better." He smiles a perfect Ken-doll smile toward me, flashing his pearly white teeth, straight and brilliant. His smile gleams like in that one toothpaste commercial.

As each moment passes talking and driving together, I begin to feel myself relax. I breathe easier. I feel less like a stress case. I guess it's because Jake has a very calming presence. His voice is even calm and reassuring.

Of course, I continue to steal looks at him because his hair is dark, like black-dark. Which, of course, is an amazing contrast to his baby blues. His eyes light up when he smiles, which literally puts me into a "he's so hot I can't handle it," semi-catatonic state.

I need to get a grip. And quickly. Clara and I had gone back and forth on my outfit choices. I settled on a skirt and blouse combo with sandals. I feel comfortable in his presence. I really like this feeling.

As we drive, we talk, and I decide to do a quick compare and contrast of myself versus Jake. Why! Idk. 'Cause I'm a dork, ha ha.

And wow. Big mistake. Here's what I come up with: so basically, I'm about a seven and he's a ten, so why the heck is Jake with me?

I pinch myself under my leg to refocus and jump right back into the convo.

"So, Hideaway Pizza? I love that place."

"I'm glad. We haven't gone yet, but I've been hearing good things about it. So, what do you do in your spare time when you don't work, do your homework, and go to school?"

"I read a lot, and I like to write poetry." Crud. I should have left that last part off. Too much information. Plus, he probably thinks I'm super lame to write poetry.

"Seriously? Poetry?"

"Yes?"

"Yes? or Yes!"

"Yes!"

He laughs and continues, "That's very cool."

My tender little heart melts into a puddle of contentment. I regain consciousness in order to ask him another question as we are approaching the restaurant, but as we turn into to the Hideway Pizza place parking lot, I suddenly gasp.

I see "her" car.

"No!" I totally screech this loudly.

Jake actually jumps in surprise. "No? What?"

"Brooke is here. Can we go somewhere else? Please?"

"Hold up. Let's see if she comes over. What's going on with you two?"

"She was waiting for me in her cute, little, shiny red Mustang when I came home from work earlier today, probing me for info about what *you* were doing tonight and also trying to get me to come with her and some other friends. She is not my friend. I'm sorry if she is your friend, but I really can't stand—"

Then she's there, coming out of Hideaway Pizza. She saunters toward Jake's car in some sort of pink ensemble, looking fantabulous. No lie. I feel like I can't breathe.

THIS JUST IN: girl almost dies of a heart attack at age seventeen, in this beautiful boy's passenger seat, of his totally sweet jeep.

Brooke comes over and pops her beautiful, flawless face right into my not-so-beautiful, definitely flaw-full face.

"Hey, you guys! Oh, my gosh, we were *just* talking about you, Jake. How come you couldn't come out with us tonight?" Her words are literally floating out of her mouth. "And wait. I thought you had to study, Gracie." Her eyes narrow and she gives a look that says, "You are SO dead girlfriend."

"Um—" I got that far because Jake rescued us both.

"My fault completely, Brooke. I was hungry and I decided to drop by and see if I could take this hard-working girl away from her studies for a while." Jake smiles his brilliant smile and Brooke visibly chills out.

"Oh, well, that's nice of you," she gives a nervous giggle after saying this.

Just then, Justin and Clara come out of Hideaway and some other dude. Oh! This is the guy Clara told me about a few weeks ago. He's in her Spanish class with her. I think it's Bo, maybe?

But I don't have time to ask 'cause Jake states firmly, but kindly to Brooke, "Have fun, Brooke. See you on Monday."

Brooke's face is one of shock and surprise, basically that *she* isn't invited. We watch as she gives us a pageant wave and walks to Justin's car. I wave to him and Clara and Bo, and they climb into the same car and pull out.

Jake turns off his Jeep, pulls out the keys, and gives me a nice smile.

"Stay put and I'll come around."

Whoa. Around to open my door?

And there he is. Opening my door, offering me his hand. I feel like Mia Thermompolos in Princess Diaries! Who does this anymore? I distinctly remember hearing time and time again that chivalry is quite dead!

Hideaway is almost always busy and noisy but so worth it, 'cause it's so delicious. While Jake asks me what I want to eat, he asks me if I would mind getting the water and grabbing us a table while he puts in our order.

"No problem," the words tumble out, but I think I must sound ridiculous.

Why do I always sound like an idiot when I speak to him? In the car I did fine. It must just be in public. It's because he is so beautiful, and I am still not sure why he is with me and not say with BROOKE? Speaking of Brooke. Am I seeing a huge lack of interest on Jake's part toward Brooke? Or am I dreaming this up!?

Jake appts me. I put my hand up. He smiles as he walks over. Mmmmm. Fried mushrooms. And a combo veggie pizza with white sauce. We eat. We talk. We laugh. It is literally the best.

I get a comfortable feeling anytime it's just us two sitting together. It's as if we're alone. Just us two like we're frozen in time. I always feel so relaxed. He's so intelligent and funny. And genuine.

Unfortunately, I let a looming question hang over me all evening. It has been on the tip of my tongue during all of our conversations. So, I just let it hang somewhere in the air, because, realistically, I don't really want to know the answer: why me and not "her?" Or even someone else for that matter? Why do I keep reciting this notion? And when will I ever just let it go and be all in and happy?

We linger at the restaurant until almost eight pm.

"Hey, Gracie, I saw that there's a Half-Price bookstore, just up the way. Is it a decent store and if so, wanna go check it out? You said you like to read, right? Me too."

"Yeah, great! Half-Price is one of my fave spots to hang." Wow.

What am I, some surfer chick? I laugh in spite of my stupidity, and give him my best, "I'm such a dork," smile.

I'm dreaming and I know it. I'm gonna wake up and it will be Brooke in my place, or some other hotty and not me, then I'll start crying like a baby as I watch them together....

"So, what do you read?"

WOAH! *Check back in Gracie. Just try to focus....*

"Oh, um, young adult fiction, classics, and mysteries."

"Awesome. I read mostly non-fiction, and some mysteries and war books."

"Excellent."

Jake surprises me again by having me stay put so he can come around and open up the door for me.

<sigh> My heart melts.

As we walk through the store, I point out the various areas of the bookstore. We talk and laugh and talk and laugh some more. I find a book I'd been looking for, so I pick it up. I tell him I was going to go buy it real, but to my surprise, he grabs it, and the one he has been holding in the crook of his arm for himself, and heads to the checkout counter.

I wander over to the vinyls and check them out, pretending like I know what I'm looking for, which I so don't. I decide I don't want to linger by Jake and feel like an idiot looking over his shoulder as he makes the purchases. I do appreciate the kind thought, though.

Suddenly, I smell a fresh scent wafting toward my nose, tantalizing my very senses.

"Ready?"

I turn around to see his amazing eyes piercing through my very soul. His face is so close to mine I actually suck in my breath. He just smiles and grabs my hand—softly, not in a bossy manner, but definitely in charge.

"So, are you up for ice cream and a walk in a park?"

"Oh, Jake, you don't have to buy me anything else, really. Dinner, a book, and now ice cream? Seriously, Jake, I'm good. You are spending too much money on me, or us, and I don't want to seem ungrateful, 'cause I really do appreciate it."

"Relax, Gracie. I wouldn't spend my money if I didn't want to. Promise. I have a lot of savings right now, so no worries, okay?"

"Okay, sure, I guess if you say so."

"Where to?"

"Have you tried Braum's yet?"

"Nope, but I'm game, so let's go! I trust your opinion completely."

He gives me a "melt in my mouth" smile and we are off.

We travel in silence for a while listening to Metric, one of my favorite groups.

"I love Metric," I say with my eyes closed. I sing along softly.

"You know this?"

"Well, yeah, my brother Zac and I share a lot of tunes together, and we all like music in my family."

"That's great." Fabulous smile flashes my way. Be still my heart!

"You have a nice voice, Gracie."

"Thanks," I say this shyly and turn my face toward the window. We decide to go through the drive-through so we can walk and eat in the park.

Ice cream purchased: rocky road for Jake and peppermint for myself, we head toward a park close to my neighborhood to finish eating.

"Great ice cream, I mean seriously!"

"Right?" I beam. Peppermint ice cream and Jake hotty? Be still my heart.

We both laugh as Jake pulls into an empty spot, then runs to my side to let me out. Once again, I think to myself that chivalry is not dead with Jake around.

I breathe in the pleasant smells as we walk toward the swings. It's slightly cooler than earlier in the day, refreshing, not frigid. We both grab a swing and start to pump as we finish eating our ice cream. As we sail back and forth, I look over at Jake, when I think he's not looking.

This boy is beautiful, kind, fun. Pinch me 'cause I'm dreaming the best darn dream ever!

"Um, Jake? Can I tell you something?" I slow my swing so I can look right at Jake.

"Sure." He follows my lead and slows down also. We both stop. I look over at him.

"I can honestly say, this has been the most relaxing time I've had, well, since my dad died. I've been working, studying, and working even more, and then taking care of stuff around the house doing so much for Mom, Beth, Zac, and me for a long, long time. I never go out, actually, never." I breathe a sigh of relief and fall silent.

I peek at him again to see what his facial expression could possibly be after my rando confession.

I don't usually act like this, but this guy is letting me feel relaxed, free and allowing me to be myself. I love feeling this way.

"I'm glad, Gracie." He winks at me.

And that's that. He starts to pump again. I follow his lead now. He starts to ask me questions.

"How's it been since you lost your dad?"

"So hard at first. Really hard. Then, as the days became weeks and the weeks became months, things slowly were less hard. Less heart wrenching. We fell into daily routines, subconsciously split up Dad's jobs, and continued to move forward."

"That's good to hear, and I'm really glad to hear that it has gotten easier and better. I'm sorry it was so hard for you all though."

"We have a wall in our dining room dedicated to Dad—childhood pictures, awkward middle school and high school pictures. Mom and Dad dating and their wedding. Us all as babies with Dad and Mom, and then their last anniversary photo, before he died."

"I would love to see your dad wall sometime."

"I would love to show you. I, um… I don't ever talk about this with anyone. Not even my BFF Clara. So, thank you for listening."

I don't tell him how I feel free like a child again, running through flower-laden fields.

"Sure." He says this softly.

"My turn for some questions."

"Shoot!"

"So, which places did you like the best where you've lived?"

"California. Definitely Cali was my favorite place. The beach. The ocean. The weather and the casual lifestyle."

"Sounds fabulous. Never been to the beach as of yet."

"Say what?"

"Never had the opportunity, I guess."

"I hope you get to go someday. It's life-changing."

"I can only imagine! Okay, next question."

CHAPTER TWELVE

*J*ake stops swinging and gestures to me to walk with him. There are park lights that light up a nice, long pathway around the entire park.

I ask my next question.

"Is it hard to make new friends?"

"Some places were harder than other places. Michigan, for example, was hard, because we were only there one year. Nebraska was better because we were there three years. California was the best spot, though. People are just chill in Southern Cali. Plus, we lived there for nearly five years. My dad says this is it. No more moves. He's tired of them. Meg and I are tired of them."

I make a note to myself that I haven't heard Jake mention his mom. Weird? Intentional? I don't know.

"Can't say I blame you one single bit. Speaking of Meg, how's she adjusting? Middle school is a bear, especially as the new kid."

"Megs is tough, thankfully, but you know, there's always that—being the new kid is rough, even for her. Beth has been a Godsend for Megs, though. Thank goodness."

"I'm so glad. I'd say the same for Beth. She's got a decent group of friends, but not one bestie. Beth says she and Meg seem to have a lot more in common than the other girls she hangs with."

"Cool. Makes me happy for her. Seriously."

"Wait. I haven't heard a thing about your mom." Crap. Did I just ask him that? Great. He probably thinks I'm so rude.

But he looks right at me and begins to talk.

"Um, Mom left my dad and us, a few years back. The moves made her crazy. She just couldn't handle it. While in Cali, she went off the deep end and left. We don't see her much."

"I am so sorry Jake. Really sorry." My voice fades at the end of my sentence.

Such a good kid for having experienced heartache. Like me, I guess.

"Me too, but like you, it was hard in the beginning, then it got easier. Either we were going to sink or swim."

"Sink or swim. Totally agree. Zac, Beth, Mom and I are the same way, I guess. Sink or swim. Guess we all eventually experience tough situations that force us to choose to sink or swim and make the best of our situations or to drag our feet, huh?"

"Sink or swim," he says with a chuckle.

I smile at him.

He continues. "I could tell you were a tough girl and a "swimmer," so to speak, right from the moment I met you, Gracie. You know what you want to do, and you do it. You're driven academically, too, and most of all, I admire how hard you work for your family. Not many kids are willing to do this anymore."

"Thanks," I whisper as I gaze out into the dark, peaceful evening.

"I'm trying to look for a job, too. Dad says if he's not going to move anymore, he will have to travel, which means I'm in charge."

"Any job leads yet?"

"A few. I'll know Monday about one job I really want. Working at the car repair place. Car and Go."

"Oh yes. We love that place. Joe's the best. That's where I took Brooke...." I trail off. I'm not going to talk about her.

"Took Brooke?"

"Well, I followed her to drop off her car. We had a fender bender at Sicily's Pizza parking lot, right after she moved here, in fact. I had to drive her to school and home again, because apparently, I'm her only friend." I sound very whiny. I sneer to myself.

"Ha, ha. Don't let Brooke get under your skin. She tries too hard. She wants everyone to like her, girls and guys alike. She needs to just chill out and be herself. Guys don't really dig the high maintenance chicks, you know. Girls think we do."

"Woah. Hold that thought and rewind! I thought guys loved all that fluff, make-up, pink everything, perfume, you know, the works!"

"Okay, some guys, but not me. I like no-nonsense. My mom's like that, too-except for her patience that just gave out.

"Well, this information is very refreshing to hear."

"I've done the same thing as you. Taken over and taken care of Meg. We have that in common. That's why I can't stand fluff. My life's too real. Like yours, I guess."

We don't say a word for what seems like forever. Just listen to the cicadas and frogs permeating the air with their natural noises.

Jake pulls his phone out.

"It's 10:45 pm. Better take you home. Wouldn't want to tick Zac off, would I, on our first date?" His eyes twinkle as he flashes me his melting smile. He grabs my hand to leads me to his Jeep. His hand is so warm—like a fresh baked roll I'm holding in my hand.

I tingle from head to toe. I never want him to let go. But then he has to, so I can get into his car. Jake lets me in and closes my door. I watch as he goes around the front of his Jeep and hops in. *Best. Night. Ever.*

He revs the gas, pulls out slowly, and grabs my hand again. Tingles. I feel like I could melt into yet another puddle of contentment. More tingles.

"So, can I talk to you tomorrow?"

He smiles as he asks this.

"Um, yeah, sure. We get back from church after noon. Then we usually eat, relax, and then we play some games. You know, Sunday family bonding."

"Cool. I'll call you when I know what I have going on."

"K." I grin a ridiculously girlish grin for the second time that evening.

Jake plugs in his iPhone. He picks Metro Boom from the new Spidey movie. I love it. My crazy roller coaster of thoughts in my mind swirl with happy and good thoughts as we hold hands and listen to the tunes.

The park is really close to my house, so it was only about a five-minute drive. But it is a most pleasant short drive. I'm feeling really happy.

In my driveway, Jake opens the car door for me, then walks me to my front door and gives me a hug goodbye.

"Thank you for a great night, Jake," I say pleasantly.

"It was a great night for me, too, Gracie. I'll text 'ya tomorrow later on, okay?"

"Sounds good. Thanks again."

And I'm through the door and already watching him as I shut the door slowly, so I can watch Jake walk to his Jeep.

You know those scenes in the movies when the girl walks into the house, shuts the door, and has that faraway, dreamy look in her eyes? This is totally me right now! I NEVER get like this. I NEVER allow myself to get like this. I like this guy, though I am still slightly suspicious and just know something could go wrong and mess it all up, but for now, I am enjoying every moment with this amazing person.

I step softly and slowly up the stairs. Mom's light is out. Beth's too. Zac's is not, so I stop in.

I knock softly on his door.

"Come in!"

"Hey. How was your night, Zac?"

"Good. Sarah came over and made us dinner. Beth ended up having Meg over, too. She's a really nice girl, and they seem to have a lot in common. Mom was finishing up a chapter, but enough about all of us! Now, spill the deets: what about you?"

I speak in a dreamy voice. "Jake is so nice. Too nice, too beautiful. It is all too good to be true, Zac. Brooke will win him over, or even some other girl. I just know it. But until that happens, I'm holding on to every moment that I have with him. We had such a good night. I feel so happy and relaxed. But Zac, he's just too perfect, and I'm just too *imperfect*." I frown and plunk myself down on Zac's bed.

"Okay, that's a little harsh, Gracie. Let's say happy things about ourselves, how 'bout? I am beautiful inside and out!" He gave me the goofiest look after saying this cheesy quote.

"Nice try. That's so cheesy and not true, you big dork."

I throw a pillow right in his face.

"Okay, but seriously, Gracie," he continued. "Let's have a little confidence in yourself, would you please? You *are a great person*, Gracie. You just don't see it. You completely sell yourself short, just to mask your feelings sometimes. Let it go. Enjoy this guy. He's into you. I saw it tonight when Jake picked you up, and Meg even talked about you."

"What? Wait, what did she even say? And, boy, do you sound just like Dad!" I smile as I say this, though, not upset, but grateful. "And wait, back to Meg, what did she say exactly?"

"That Jake likes you. Period."

"Cool, cool, cool. Very cool...." my voice trickles off somewhere into my new favorite spot: Dreamville.

"Yep. So, lighten up, let it go, and let it happen, will 'ya? Now, scoot, 'cause I gotta go to bed. But I wanted to wait up for my little sis, you know."

"Thanks," I shut his door quietly, smiling with a warm assurance of two things: I love my brother Zac and maybe Jake *did* like me a little more than I gave myself credit for.

As per my typical nightly routine, I text Clara for a check in. She'd texted me a bit ago while I was talking with Zac.

'Best date ever.'

'Omg spill'

'Dinner-bookstore-ice cream-park.'

'Amaze.'

'He is so nice and smart and beautiful.'

'Wow-fabulous-I am so happy for u.'

'How about your night?'

'Things going super well with Bo. He's the best!'
'So, so glad-night night bestie c u at church tm.'
I wash my face and brush my teeth so fast 'cause I am so tired, but a happy tired. I fall into bed—tonight, I pop in my ear pods and drift off to Dreamville once again….

CHAPTER THIRTEEN

*S*un seeps into my window, glaring into my eyes as I remove my sleeping mask and slothfully attempt to get out of bed… with no success.

Church. Gotta get up.

I am still very sleepy, because I want to return to my dreams of Jake and me….

I roll over and look at my clock—8:15am! Crap!

I fly out of bed—I seem to be doing this a lot—I run the shower and get ready as fast as possible. My heart was all a flutter with every thought of Jake. But tucked in the dark corners of my mind were also those doubts—what if? A Prettier girl? A better girl? I push them out.

For now, I will try to enjoy this small happiness.

As I'm trotting down the stairs, phone in hand, I feel my phone buzz. A text. So early? I am afraid to look.

"It's probably Brooke."

But it was Jake. Ahhhh… my heart is never going to survive this emotional entourage of good feelings!

'Hey, you up? Have some family stuff, but then can Meg and I drop over after 3ish?'

YES!! I want to scream. I about lose my balance in my heels as I negotiate the last few steps, while trying to text him back.

'That would be great! Thanks for last night. So much fun.'

I hope that wasn't too overkill.

'Ditto-See ya later.'

Who can concentrate in church when you feel like your heart is about to burst? I try, I really do. But, by noon, I'd been ready since I got to church, so I am more than ready to get home, and STAT.

It's my turn to make lunch. Mom is on dinner for today. We decided a while back to lessen Mom's burden by switching between all of us in our meal prep duties.

"Well, my beauties," Mom says with a huge grin. "My book is finally done. I have submitted it to Kenneth, my editor, and now will be gearing up to do my most favorite part: working on any and all revisions and red marks that needed fixing!" She shares this statement with us oozing with sarcasm.

This part usually takes a few weeks, and then it's off to the printer! She has been working night and day, but, today, she is taking a well-deserved and a most needed break with us. I make grilled cheese sandwiches and tater tots, and we have pears from a can. Real gourmet, I know.

Hey, at least I fix something edible and with a fruit!

We decide to play Boggle right after lunch today, since I had previously asked everyone if they were okay if Jake and Meg came over to hang with us after three today. Sarah is always hanging with Zac at our house, so that's nothing new, so I figure, what's two more people?

Mom is going to go over to a friend's house later until dinnertime, so the day is turning out to be very pleasant for everyone.

I have just loaded in the last of the dishes, wiped the counters down, lit a simple fragranced candle, and am just starting the dishwasher when I hear Beth yell, "Hey Gracie, they're here!"

I hear Meg's sweet voice as Beth answers the door and lets them both in. Meg's a tall, lanky dark-haired beauty. And boy, is she so kind. Like her brother. Uncanny, seeing as how their mom bailed on them. You'd think they'd have some bitterness, but nope! That's my favorite quality in her, well, in anyone for that fact.

I casually wait a whole whopping two minutes and then walk through the doorway that connects the kitchen and family room. I try to come across as very nonchalant, but the moment I see Jake's soul-melting, blue eyes, mercy–he looks so very hot! Pink shirt, hair tousled, faded jeans. He's tall, too, well over six feet. My heart palpitates. I feel heat rush to my cheeks!

Get a grip!

I breathe slowly and count to twenty quickly and luckily, I manage to keep myself together. I'm even wearing a new, but casual, sundress I forgot I hadn't worn yet. My hair is already curly, because we dress up for church on Sundays, so bonus for me.

"Hey, Meg, I'm Gracie. It's so nice to finally meet you!"

"Nice to finally meet *you*. I've heard so much about you, all good of course." Firm grip, same blue eyes as Jake and so darling.

Jake elbows her in the ribs.

"Ow! Jake, sheesh!" Meg cracks up while feigning being injured and grasps her side.

"Thanks Meg," he says through smiling barred teeth.

"Meg, what say you and I go upstairs and watch a movie in my room? Flixnet has some new movies we can check out." Beth says happily.

"Great. Bye, you two." Raucous giggles follow Meg and Beth as they run up the stairs.

"Sorry, that was a little awkward, huh?"

"Just a bit," I smile. "Come on into the front room. Wanna watch TV? A movie? Play a game? Listen to music?"

"Whatever is good with me," Jake grins warmly.

He follows me into the front room. Mom has left a little bit ago but will be back in a few hours. Zac had said hello and goodbye when Jake and Meg showed up. Off to Sarah's house. Some family birthday celebrations for a distant relative of Sarah's.

Jake sits down on the couch. I sit by him, but not exactly right by him. I'm still so nervous. I can feel the fire in my cheeks again like flames! Jake grabs a photo book under the table. It was mine, of course, and starts flipping through it.

"Can I look at it?"

"Uh...."

"Come on, Gracie."

He opens the book. Nothing like awkward pics of you when you're little to break the awkwardness!

"It's you! Ah, aren't you so cute!" He says this with obvious sarcasm and pinches my cheek.

"Ha, ha. Very funny. Mmmm, maybe I should ask Meg to bring me *your* baby book then I can mock *you* openly?" I laugh.

"Oh, but you really were so darn cute. And look how you've grown up and you're so pretty."

I stare at him. "Right."

Did I just say that out loud?

"You are, silly girl." He keeps flipping the pages and asks questions. He doesn't even skip a beat.

"What age were you here?"

I peer at the picture for a minute.

"Oh, yes, I'm ten years old. At my grandma's farm." The scene of that day suddenly rushes into my mind and a content smile creeps onto my lips. We picked peaches, made pie, rode on the tractor—oh, it was one of my favorite days. I always love that pictures have the power to trigger fond memories, washed over by a wave of emotion and tender thoughts. Amazing.

"Oh, wait, this picture is you from last year, I guess?"

"Ew, yes. Okay, let's play a game or watch something, please? I really hate photos."

"But you're very photogenic, Gracie. Really nice." He looks at me. I turn pink, fuchsia, or maybe red, I don't even know for sure.

"Wanna play cards?" I get up rapidly. I'm completely flustered.

"Something to eat? Drink, perhaps?"

I cringe. Could I be any more of an awkward dork right now? What is wrong with me? Seriously!

I walk into the kitchen. Meg and Beth were popping microwave popcorn.

"Um, Gracie, why are you so pink?"

"Thank you, Beth, for bringing that to my attention—um, I'm sunburnt?"

"You haven't even been in the sun...."

"REALLY? Are you SURE?" Sarcasm oozes in a crazed whisper with every word.

"It's Jake, isn't it?"

"STOP. Now!" I glare at her like only a sister can glare at a sibling.

I then flash her a warning look that her death is looming over her head if she says one. More. Word!

"Beth, be nice," Meg chimes in.

"Okay. Let's go Meg. Sheesh, Gracie, relax already!" And they're gone. I pour two glasses of milk and haphazardly fling some cookies on a plate.

Chocolate chip cookies could definitely help me go back into face the most beautiful boy I've ever met.

Oh crap! I think I'm feeling hot—again!

"Okay, just breathe, Gracie!" I chide myself. I count to fifty then walk in pretending to be calm and casual.

"So, I make you nervous in the daylight apparently?" He laughs. He takes a glass of milk from me and two cookies. I have nothing to say. I just grin sheepishly and shrug my shoulders.

"Did you start your book? I did." I begin. ANYTHING to make the awkwardness go away! "Thanks again for buying it for me," I continue, and then bow my head shyly. I must sound like such a loser!

Jake puts his hand under my chin and lifts my head. He looks into my eyes.

"Your eyes are so green. Truly beautiful."

"Cards?" I grab a deck. I'm obvi not okay with people paying any attention to me, at all. I like to work hard, keep busy and stay out of any limelight. Jake is trying to make me crazy! But, in a good way.

Ping! We get a text simultaneously.

"Brooke just asked what I'm doing right now."

"Me too!"

"She wants to hang out and is lonely and bored!"

I make a sad face.

"And we will both text her back and say we are busy, sorry, and that we'll see her at school on Monday."

"Okay."

We send our texts.

No response from Brooke.

"She's going to be mad at us both tomorrow at school!"

"She'll survive," he retorts sarcastically.

Jake makes a funny face, and I grab the cards and start dealing them out between us both.

"Okay, how about a couple games of speed?"

"Sure, Gracie, then let's take a walk, okay?"

"Yeah, sure."

Of course he won three times. I won once, since my emotions were like a ship in a storm at sea. We finish our milk and cookies, grab our phones. and start for the door. Jake grabs my hand, ever so gently, and leads us out. Twitter-pated doesn't even describe the electricity that flows through my whole being. It is so amazing I can feel this way.

WOW.

If I could just be silent and not be so awkward and lame when I am around Jake, I'd be golden! I could just smile and keep silent.

He keeps a hold of my hand out the door, down the sidewalk and all the way as we start to walk around down the sidewalk and to the park in my neighborhood.

CHAPTER FOURTEEN

J take periodic peeks at him as we discuss multiple topics. Our conversation flows naturally, but my mind can barely keep up with all of my feels. Jake is simply so easy to talk to!

"Your neighborhood is really pleasant. How long have you lived here?"

"Going on ten years now. Once my dad switched jobs, we moved here to Katy. It has been such a sweet little city to live in.

Before I know it, we've circled the block and are facing my cute, yellow house, when suddenly I feel Jake tugging me down onto the lawn. He pats his hand to signal for me to sit beside him under our large, pink-blossomed crepe myrtle tree. I blush and let him pull me down.

"Gracie," he starts, "I like that I can talk to you, about anything. I like that you blush all the time around me. It's really cute. I also like that you actually like me for everything else but my looks."

If he only knew how hot I think he is, he'd laugh right now, but I do love to talk with him about everything.

"Ha, I'm so sorry that I'm so ridiculous!"

"But you're not. You're so cute when you do that. So kind. So pretty. You make me happy. I mean I know it's just been a few weeks that we've known each other, but It's been a pretty hard year for Meg and me, as you well know, and you know how other girls can be. Take Brooke for example...."

His face scrunches up in a pained look.

Holy! I would've never guessed he felt that strongly about her in that way. Not at all!

"She looks at me and sees my looks. That's it. She's more interested in what I look like *with* her then she is interested in *who* I am. It's cool. Happens a lot. I just remain friendly and keep my distance. Brooke is a very persistent person though. Very."

"Yes. She. Is. And can I just say that I can't believe you even talked to me, what with Blondie Clone Girl. Oh, my gosh! I mean Brooke sitting in front of me?" I blush again.

"Blondie Clone Girl? That's pretty funny and actually quite accurate–she does look like a clone. And for your information Gracie, I spotted you right away that first day I came to class. You weren't even looking at me, in fact you ran into me with your backpack and ran out of class. You made me laugh. I remember thinking to myself, a pretty girl like that not even noticing me? Excellent!"

"Excellent?!"

"Yes. I want to be liked for me, for who I am, for what I can offer this world and NOT for my blue eyes or my face. It's maddening." He breaks off his sentence abruptly. He has grabbed a handful of grass and is flinging each piece up into the air as he's talking to me.

Meanwhile in my head, I'm saying to myself: Eyes? What eyes? YOU have eyes? I've never even noticed your big, blue, gorgeous eyes. And your face? Not one bit!

"Anyway, when I was in Latin that first day, you were so real to me. I appreciated that, and I was immediately attracted to you for that very fact. I think you were even a little sarcastic, yeah, if I remember, you were sort of put out by having to help me. It was great. "

"Great, huh. Well, how about you scared me to death! You, so beautiful and good looking and talking to me? And wanting to study with me? Pfff."

"Come on now. You so don't give yourself credit. You are so pretty and smart," his comment floats into the wind as Zac and Sarah drive up. But I heard it.

We watch as Zac helps open the door for Sarah.

"Such a good brother you have, Gracie."

"Agreed," I smile and introduce everyone around.

"Sarah, this is Jake, Jake, Zac's girlfriend Sarah Peters."

"Pleasure." Jake had risen to his feet to shake her hand.

"You guys wanna come in and watch a movie and have some cake and ice cream? Sarah's mom sent it with us."

"Sure, yeah, great," Jake and I answer in unison.

Jake reaches his hand down to me. I grab it, happily, and he pulls me up with his very strong grip. He follows me into my house. I show him into the family room once again and join Zac in the kitchen. He and I dish the ice cream and cake, while Jake and Sarah get better acquainted in the other room.

"So, sis, how are things going with you and Jake?"

"We are just, um, friends…." I try to hide my eyes from Zac.

"Ha! Yeah, right."

"No! Really. We see!" I look at him with innocent puppy eyes. He was not even going for it.

"Yeah, yeah." He laughs. "You guys seem to mesh really well. I see the way he looks at you. I know this looking because I def look at Sarah like that." Zac winks at me.

"Okay, yeah. I guess, it seems like he likes me. I mean, I sure as heck know how I feel about him! He's so nice, Zac. Smart. Beautiful. Like I said the other night. He is very complimentary of me, and I always blush and know I don't deserve such compliments."

"Sis! Will you kindly drop! I mean, will 'ya? Look, as a dude, if I don't dig a girl, I won't give any time to her. He likes you. Go with it."

"Okay. I still get so nervous and twitter-pated around him. I am so, I don't know…."

"I think it is called, 'diggin him, little sis.'"

"Ha. You're cute!" But my smile says enough to answer him. I am SO diggin' Jake. Big time. Dinner dished onto my favorite Daisy patterned plates, we walk into the dining table area together. Sarah and Jake both look up as we enter. They smile so it seems they have been having a dec conversation and are now ready to eat and to start a movie.

I move in to sit by Jake. Zac does the same and sits by Sarah. It is good to have my brother and Sarah here. They have dated for over a year, so she is practically part of the family now. Zac pops in one of our fav movies, *She's the Man*. Tame, but funny and romantic. Dinner consumed. Zac has dished us all up some cake that Beth and Maddy made earlier today. With ice cream to top it off. Mm. We eat our cake while laughing at the movie. My phone buzzes. Crap. Not again. It's freaking Brooke. I read her text and frown.

'Why are you taking Jake away from me? You know I like him. A lot. I thought you knew this and would leave Jake alone for my sake.'

I feel like I've just been stung by a bee. These stupid words hurt my heart. And, how am I to even answer? What I say to a text such as this? So cruel. So mean. So selfish. I growl within my very soul. I end up not sending any response.

Jake suddenly notices the frown on my face and whispers into my ear, "Who is it? You look upset."

"Oh, wrong number. I'm good." I lie.

"You sure?"

"Yep! So good!"

He eyes me and doesn't seem terribly convinced so I just turn toward the TV and pretend to be deeply engrossed in the movie.

I settle myself close to Jake, and to my pleasant surprise, he puts his strong arm around me. I try to relax, by snuggling in even a bit closer to him. He smells divine, and despite feeling broken hearted from Brooke's text, I begin to relax, again, like Saturday night. He really has a calming aura about him. I truly love this about him.

As the credits scroll down, I hear a car pull in. I shrug it off because It's probably Mom. But then there's a knock at the door. Zac gets up to answer it.

"Gracie, it's for you." He yells at me.

I get up, not knowing who to expect. Oh, my gosh. My facial expression drops. It's Brooke. No kidding. I'm feeling a bit terrified and decide it's best to just step outside onto the front porch to speak with her.

"Hey, Brooke, what's up?" I ask, trying to not give off any vibes of the actual fear and trepidation that is running through my bloodstream.

"Oh, hey. I was in the area, so I just wanted to stop by." This is said in her sugary tone.

"Okay, cool, so, what can I do for you?"

"I assume you got my text?" Now this comes out quite harsh.

But unbeknownst to my own self, a sneaky wave of super-slyness washes over me, and I decide I will lie. I don't even know where this stuff is coming from! So. Not. Me.

"Text? What text?"

"I sent you a text concerning a certain someone, named Jake. Ring a bell?" Even more harshly said.

"Nope, not one bit. I've been watching a movie, sorry." Innocently spoken.

My lie is actually making me feel stronger and empowered.

"We never get to hang out, especially now that my car is fixed." She sort of whined this out. Most annoying. Like she's thinking we were friends at some point? Um, that's a nope.

I blurt out, "Yeah, well, we do get to see each other in English, remember? And in choir?" I try super hard to have this sound sort of upbeat. Like I actually care about her. Which. I. Do. Not.

"Sure, silly, but I meant outside of school, ha ha, oh and on another note, I've been trying to get a hold of Jake, you haven't seen him, have you? He never seems to have much time to respond to my texts. Maybe I don't have his number right? It's so weird."

It's at this frightening point that I realize she has been looking 'round and yep! You got it. She sees Jake's Jeep parked under one of our crepe myrtle tree overhanging our curb.

"Wait. Is that his car over there? Is he HERE? With YOU?"

I'd like to share with you right now that I think I see actually little flames of anger light up in her eyes!

"Well, yeah, actually, he stopped by with his sister because my sister and his sister are really good friends, and—"

"Just save it. I don't want to hear any more of your lies. I am so furious. And I can't believe he's here with YOU. To be honest, I thought we were better friends than this. I told you it was *Jake* I want, and no one else, and here you are WITH him."

She growls at me and flies off the front porch stairs and is stomping to her car. She turns before getting into her driver's side and gives me a death glare. It sends chills down my spine. I never even got to attempt to respond because of her rapid and furious stomps to her car.

Oh, week! I'm supes glad I didn't have to respond. She roars out of the driveway. I turn 'round and grab the doorknob softly and try and sneak back inside and quietly close the door behind me.

I will be the first to admit a rise of fear is still lingering over me, and even though Jake is obviously here with me, Brooke seems to be on a warpath to prove to me how very insignificant I am.

Well, she's doing a good job.

CHAPTER FIFTEEN

"Who was that Gracie?" This is Jake asking me this question.

"Just a friend. Told her I was busy."

"Kind of sounded like Brooke."

"Yeah, okay, well, yeah, it was her. Anyways, who's up for a smashing game of UNO?"

But I can tell immediately as Jake is practically peering into my souls that he sure isn't going to let this go.

"Gracie, you up for a walk around the block again? Or maybe to that park nearby?"

I grin at him and rise to indicate my acceptance of his suggestion.

"We'll be back in just a bit guys, okay?"

Zac and Sarah nod. They are in some sort of discussion, so this works out perfectly.

Once outside, Jake takes my hands and steers me in front of him. "Okay. Let's go. Spill. What the heck is going on?"

One look into his ocean-blue eyes, and tears fill my eyes and spill down my cheeks. He pulls me into a hug. He's warm and comforting. I feel like an idiot

Crying into his cute sweatshirt, but Jake holds me close. So, I have a good cry. My heart is literally bursting with sadness. I don't like to say this phrase, but I do believe so truly hate Brooke!

I am calming down enough so that I can pull back and I begin to "spill," all the deets as we walk.

"That text I got earlier? Yeah. It *was* from Brooke. "

"What the heck does she want from you?"

"She's soooo mad. At *me*. Because *you* are hanging with me. She says she texts you, but you don't respond. And she has been relentless about how I'm so plain and boring—she's so mean to me. She's going to ruin everything for me, for us...."

I know without a doubt that Brooke could take my happiness and completely and utterly destroy it and squash my heart into tiny, invisible shattered pieces strewn all over the ground—splat!

Jake squeezes my hand as we approach the park.

"No, she's not. And no she won't. She can say and do what she wants, but WE can too. Brooke talks a good game, but she's just as human as we are, well, she's a bit like a mean-girl clone girl, but you know."

This makes me laugh. We sit close on a bench together. I let out a content sigh. He puts his arm around me, and I rest my head on his strong shoulder. We stay like this for a while. As we sit there, he speaks softly to me and continues to reassure me, saying things like Brooke can be as mean as she wants, but that she certainly has no control of whom we hang out with, nor date, and other words of encouragement.

Date? Did he say date? My stomach jumps with excitement. I soooo want to "date" this amazing boy more than he knows, but I know we are just starting out, so I can be patient if the end result is to be with Jake.

We saunter back, holding hands, talking about this, that, and the other. It's almost 8:30 pm by the time we get back to my house. We both realize we need to get on our homework. Jake walks me right to my door and gives me a long, tender hug.

Be still my heart.

"See 'ya tomorrow, Gracie!" He smiles his twenty-four-watt smile and winks at me with his magical eyes. "Oh! I almost forgot Meg, ha ha."

"I'll grab her. And Jake, um, thanks for a great day." I smile and open the door and yell, "Meg! Time to go, sweetie. Jake is waiting in the Jeep for 'ya."

Meg bounds happily down the stairs. "Bye, Beth. Bye, Gracie!"

I close the door slowly watching her as Jake lets her in the Jeep and as he reverses out of our driveway and heads down the street to his house.

I close the door and lean against it, and I sigh.

MONDAY COMES WAY TOO QUICKLY. I AM EXCITED TO SEE JAKE AND terrified to see Brooke. She was so mean yesterday. I dreamt about her being very large and I was very small, and she kept trying to smash me with her giant foot! It was horrid.

I slither into my seat in Language Arts as quickly as I can, open my book and begin reading.

Ugh, I can smell her even before she takes her seat.

"Well, good morning, boy-stealer. How are you feeling about being so cruel?" She pouts these words out and I feel somewhat nauseated.

I choose to take the high road and ignore her rudeness. She turns around brushing me, my book, and my desk with her hair.

Gonna be a great day! I think sarcastically.

Luckily, she's just trying to get Jake's attention all of class, so I'm spared any more interactions. Phew!

Unfortunately, any time I see Brooke throughout the day, she is talking to someone about Jake or TO Jake, as I pass by their classes. I can hear her ridiculously loud conversations permeate through all the walls, doors and windows. I try to keep calm. Try is the key word here.

I only have Latin with Jake. I don't even have the same lunch block. It's dreadful! Thankfully, Brooke IS NOT in Latin. I'm so grateful to make it to last period and I anxiously sit down and await his arrival.

I feel his closeness before he leans over my shoulder and whispers, "Hey, beautiful!"

I nearly bash into Jake's perfect face, but luckily, he, being the more coordinated of the two of us, sits down and, of course, laughs at me and kisses my cheek. I immediately blush. I'm not used to PA, especially when it's MY PA! I turn and look at him and butterflies commence to do an immense amount of fluttering in my tummy.

<sigh>

I breathe in a relaxing breath and smile right back at him.

We've got a few minutes before the bell rings, and I can see his bursting at the seams with convo to share with me.

"Boy, and what a day I've had with Clone Girl. Holy cow, she's been all over me, talking to me, and basically stalking me."

"Oh, I know. I heard her anytime I passed by your classes. Sheesh!

"Well, today she's gone overboard with her behavior. She's been really pushy, too. I'm going to have to talk to her, I guess. Seriously. She's out of line now. On a less stressful note, are you working tonight?"

"Yes, I am!" I say this cheerfully because it's a happy place for me.

"Care to study for our Latin test later, maybe at my house?"

"I'd love it!"

"Great. I can come and pick you up or you could head over after work—whichever."

"I'll head to you. Think Megs would like Beth to come, too?"

"I'll text her and see and let you know after school."

Jake squeezes my hand and we continue our task at hand. I just can't hardly wait until school is over, when I get to spend time with this beautiful boy.

Of course, these pleasant thoughts are rudely interrupted by a little storm cloud on my sunshiny day—and the cloud is named Brooke. She seems to be everywhere today. No lie. In the hall, in the bathroom, in the library, and NOW waiting by my vehicle. The girl is relentless!

Okay, I know that what I chose to do next is way out of character for me, but I just can't help myself today. She's making me crazy!

"Hey, Brooke. Sorry! Can't chat, gotta go to work!" I jump in my truck rapidly and haul off.

I dare to peek into my rearview mirror and am not surprised to see a flabbergasted look on Brooke's face. I mean, I would have looked the same way, but I don't care a lick. I am so over this mean girl crap. OVER IT.

I fly through our front door. Flit up the stairs, change quickly, and descend again. I stop in the kitchen and Mom's in there.

"Hey, Mom," I give her a quick hug. "I'm off to work!"

"I think these are the only words I've heard from you in the last three days!"

"Ha ha, well, *someone* was having a good time with her publisher here and there," I laugh warmly.

"True, I have. Kenneth's so great…. Anyway, hearing good things about this boy Jake, do tell me more."

I look up to see a dreamy look on her sweet face. She really digs this guy! She's still in the kitchen with me as I'm making a PB and J.

"He's amazing." These words flutter out of my mouth with true sincerity.

"Amazing, hmmmm, how?" My mom is giving me that mom-look of SPILL all the deets.

"He's kind, caring, beautiful, smart, kind…."

"Ha ha. Sounds like a keeper to me. And what I've seen of him, I am very impressed with him. He's a great guy."

"Oh, he totally is. So sorry Mom, it's so good to talk, Mom, miss you! Gotta go. Oh! Could I study at Jake's house after? Beth can come with me because she and Meg have some project they're working on. I'll just swing by after my shift."

"Sure, just be sure to text when you and Beth get to Jake's, okay? Oh, and please make sure either his dad or mom are there."

"Of course, mother, sheesh! And it's just the two kids and their dad. The mom left. Really sad."

"Aw, that's terrible. I'm sorry to hear that."

She smiles and gives me a quick hug.

"See 'ya."

"See 'ya, darlin'."

My shift goes until only eight pm. Busy, fun, and it really felt shorter than usual, since I work my head off, and most of all because I get to see Jake at the end of my shift.

As I say my good-byes, and as I am about to literally put my hand on the door of Sicily's and walk out, there's Brooke. No kidding. She pulls up to the curb and puts down her window.

"Uh-oh."

I was aiming to be at Jake's by 8:30 pm, and I need to still go by my house and grab Beth. I obviously don't have much to say to her and don't want to be detained.

"Hey, Gracie!" Brooke yells from her rolled down window.

"Hey, Brooke." I walk in a beeline to big blue in the opposite direction. No time to chat–darn! But Brooke, apparently, has other intentions. I'm at my truck when suddenly she is too!

"Where are you going? To meet Jake?" She hisses his name off her lips and not in a kind or friendly way.

"Yes, I am, as a matter of fact." The words come out more boldly than I felt had in me.

"Well, like, what are you two dating or something? As if he would even go for you, pfff," she announces with obvious disdain.

"And why not?" I say right back to her.

"Why not? Well, you're, well, so plain looking and dress soooo boring–duh!"

"Gee thanks, Brooke."

"Well, Jake is so gorgeous and... obviously, I am too, and well, you're just not."

With those mean and hideous words, she has crossed the line with me, and she's the mean, evil girl that I have always figured her to be. I am seething now. And tears begin to well in my eyes.

I can feel myself getting hot—with anger and sadness.

CHAPTER SIXTEEN

"I have to go." My soul is feeling wrecked.

I slam the truck door in her beautiful and flawless face and the tears slowly trickle down my cheeks. I rev the engine, back out, and take off. I screech out of the parking lot, careful not to hit her precious Camaro or anyone else.

I cry all the way home. My heart physically hurts. Why does Brooke think she deserves everything, especially Jake? Why is she so mean to me? Who does she think she is? I wipe my tears as I pull into our driveway.

I text Beth so she can come out. I look at myself in the rear-view mirror. Mascara has stained my cheeks. I lick my finger and wipe it as best as I can. My phone beeps.

'Coming sis!'

Beth runs out with such a beautiful smile on her pretty face. I make sure the doors are unlocked so she can get into the truck. Fortunately, it's dark in the truck, so Beth can't see my reddened eyes. I play like all is just swell as we exchange pleasantries.

"Hey sis, how are 'ya?

"Awesome! And you?"

"Good shift at work, so can't complain. Oh, we can't stay too late tonight, obviously. School night and all."

"Yeah, no prob."

I flip on the radio to drown out the aching in my heart. Jake and Meg live about ten minutes away, so the drive is short. I don't like to share my tears with anyone, so I hope my face and eyes are getting back to normal.

Hesitantly, I park on the curb. Beth jumps out, whereas I slowly open my door and climb out. I look up as I am shutting my door to see Jake standing on his doorstep. His smile is so sincere. But my heart is hurting. My head hurts because I cried so hard, and especially as I recall the words Brooke said to me earlier.

I can't stop thinking about her hideous words.

I grab my backpack, take one more look in the mirror, and get out of Old Blue.

"Welp, here goes," I sigh quietly to myself.

Beth had been in the house for like three minutes by the time I walk to the front doorstep.

"Hey, Gracie, how was your shift?"

"Great. Did you have to work?" I can't even think! I try to fake a happy voice, but I sound depressed.

"Better now." Luckily, Jake didn't seem to notice. Or at least, I am hoping he didn't notice.

"Come on in, let's get going on our lovely Latin. Are you hungry?"

"No, I'm good, thanks." I had been starved but have lost my appetite at this point.

I follow Jake into his house. It's clean and simply decorated. I like it a lot. We end up in his kitchen and I take a seat at the table. Well, Jake pulls the chair out for me to take a seat. He has a few water bottles and some chips out.

I pull my Latin book out, my pencil and spiral. As I am doing this, I realize that Jake is staring at me with a concerned look.

"What's going on, Gracie?"

"N-nothing at all. I'm good."

"Nice try." He takes my hand from across the table. And then the tears fall like raindrops on dry land.

"What happened, Grace? Can you tell me?" His voice is so sweet. So kind.

"Brooke…."

Jake's face starts to turn red, and he looks mad. "What did she do now? That girl, grrrrr."

"It's nothing, really." I sniff and wipe some tears from my cheeks and chin.

"Nothing? Tears don't mean just nothing, Gracie."

I know. It's not just nothing, it's something and my heart is broken.

I close my eyes and breathe in, then out.

"She pulled up right as I got off work tonight. I tried to walk away, and then there she was. Right by my truck. And then she proceeds to tell me how I'm plain and boring and that she's gorgeous like you and that you and she should be together, not you and me."

"What in the world? She's crazy. I mean, please, where does she get off saying that crap to you?" He's so upset.

I lower my head. I feel defeated and the tears come cascading down my cheeks once more. Jake is still holding my hand, and he pulls me up out of my seat and into him. He's so tall, so strong, and just, well, wonderful.

He holds me close and I cry a bit more. And then, he nuzzles his mouth into my hair and kisses my head. It is sweet. I feel myself begin to calm down. I start to pull away so I can wipe my eyes and my nose, but he holds me close again.

I relax and bury my head into his shoulder. What have I done to deserve this boy in my life? We both sort of pull away at the same time. He hands me a Kleenex box. I try to restore myself to look somewhat normal and wipe away any tears that may remain and makeup mess off of my face. I take a few deep breaths and sit back down. Jake sits, too.

"Do you think you can concentrate enough to do our Latin and then we can talk again? I'm so sorry, Gracie, about Brooke's unkindness toward you. It makes me so angry. I have to calm myself down before I can even talk about what Clone Girl did to you. Know that it's not okay with me, and it shouldn't be okay with you either."

I smile.

"I do feel better. Thanks Jake. And yeah. I just want to forget about all of it!"

We dig into our Latin. Thankfully, we both are very competent in Latin, so studying is more fun than tedious. I feel pretty good throughout the entire next hour, until I get a text. And it's Brooke.

"Okay, this is too much for me to handle now. I'm done."

"Who is it? Brooke? Seriously? Let me see your phone."

'I'm watching you Gracie.'

"Good grief! What is she, some psycho stalker? Want me to text something back to her?" he asks.

"No! It's fine. I don't want to even read her stupid texts, nor answer them. She's gone way too far with me now. Way too far. In fact, I'm ignoring her now."

"Fair enough. Just ignore her. Good call."

"Thanks for being so kind, Jake, and for taking the time to study with me. I do feel a lot better, even after the Clone Girl's latest text."

"Are you sure?" He looks pleadingly into my eyes.

"I'm sure." I look right back into his delicious eyes.

Jake squeezes my hand and holds it for a few minutes. Firework sensations and tingles shoot through me. I really like this boy. Like really a lot.

School days have now become completely tainted by Clone Girl. I love to learn and study, but my love of learning is now getting ruined by my loathing and hatred toward Blondie Clone Mean Girl! Every day she shimmies into ELAR and every day she lets her ridiculously sweet-smelling hair sweep across my desk. On purpose. And she never lets a moment pass without a snarky, rude comment uttered from her perfectly pink lips.

(Remember that one or two times I mentioned she MIGHT be different from the other clone girl types and that she was even nice? Well scratch that. Burn those words. She's actually exactly as I figured she'd be.)

"Well, good morning, plain Jane. Oh, looks like you put some lip gloss on today. Nice effort. I didn't know you even knew how to apply makeup." She giggles and turns 'round in her seat.

I just grit my teeth. If I say something, it won't matter. She'll always have another mean thing to say to me. Sigh. But I really DO want to stand up and scream at her to leave me alone forever. Wish I had the guts to do that.

This same ritual has gone on for many weeks: snarky words. Mean giggles. And then the sweeping of the hair across my desk and book. As her hair sweeps my desk this time, I fling it off of the top of my desk, and scoot back.

Brooke turns around and stares at me.

"Knock it off, will 'ya?" I say this with obvious disdain.

"What? I'm doing nothing." She smiles evilly.

"Leave. Me. Alone. Please."

"I'm doing nothing, I don't even know what you're talking about."

"Stop texting me. Stop stalking me. Stop being so mean to me too." I can't believe these words are coming out of MY MOUTH. But obviously, I've had enough of her.

I glare at her with a newfound boldness. A miracle. She has nothing to say and turns around and faces the front. Mr. McFadden looks at me with a weird facial expression. I give him a thumbs up and he shrugs.

I can't believe I just did that. Me. Gracie-Ann spoke like that to a Clone Girl? What the heck was going on inside my brain? I feel empowered though, and I guess I'm done giving in to dumb Clone Girls' meanness. I like Jake and I'm going to fight for him.

I walk to my next class. My thoughts swirl around like a tornado of strength and anger mixed. I don't even know how I will make it through the day, but my main goal is to try to avoid Blondie at all possible costs. I just focus on making it to Latin class. And Jake.

I sigh in relief as I enter the classroom. He's there before me. Hallelujah! I walk to my seat, pull it out, and sit down, thumping my books on my desk.

"Rough day?" Jake smiles and winks at me.

"Well, you could say that."

"What happened?"

"I chewed out Brooke in ELAR this morning. She was pulling the mean girl crap, saying awful things again, and I just lambasted her!"

"You did what?" He high-fived me. "Good for you, Gracie. Good. For. You."

"I guess, yes, it was good, I just felt like a crazy person had taken me over, but you know—" We're interrupted by our Latin teacher. "Okay, everyone, let's get into our groups and be ready to present your group projects today."

I whisper, "We'll talk after class." I smile at him.

He brushes my cheek with his hand. I melt inside. Is it possible to have your insides melt? 'Cause mine do every time he looks at me or touches me. I sigh contentedly and get to work.

Presentations went well. I was relieved. Check! Another thing off of my list of life!

After school, Jake usually walks me to my car. this is one of my favorite rituals we share together. When we get to Old Blue, he hugs me goodbye and I climb into my truck. Home

Sweet home. Snack. Off to work!

When I arrive at home, no one is there today. I grab some food and write a quick note on the family whiteboard.

"I'm at work until eight!"

I lock up and then climb back into my truck. It's hard to concentrate because of the thoughts whizzing through my mind as I drive to work:

"I am glad to be going to work tonight. I need some positive vibes from Julie and the rest of my work peeps. I remember seeing Brooke drive away from the school parking lot. She had a death stare on her face as she glared at me, since Jake was holding my hand as he walked me to old blue. He hadn't kissed me—yet—but I am fine with this. I don't want all the amazing sensations of hand holding and looking into his azure ocean-colored eyes to disappear, because I am pretty sure when he kisses me, I am going to keel over in happiness. Sappy, I know.

"Gracie!" Both Shaun and Julie greet me with big smiles and warm hugs. I love these people. I love working Friday night, actually, too. It's so great to see many regulars and to be so busy. Time passes quickly when you're working your fingers to the bone!

"So, what's up with you, Gracie?" Julie and I were in the back taking a quick break during a much-needed lull in the steady traffic flow that had continued all night long.

"Nothin' really."

"I'm sensing something, actually. Wanna talk?"

"Basically, there's an amazing new boy that moved in and he's actually interested in ME." I say this with notable emphasis.

"Oh, that's so great, and hardly a shocker. You don't give yourself enough credit darlin'."

"Well, you're sweet, but you're my boss!"

Her look made me smile. I knew she meant it.

"But there's this girl. I call her Blondie Clone girl 'cause she SO looks like a clone of that popular doll, anyway, she's been ruthless and terribly mean about Jake. She fawns all over him at school and she says awful things to me like he couldn't possibly like me 'cause I'm so plain and on and on...."

My voice fades. I feel tears well up in my eyes.

"Good grief! What's wrong with people?" She pulls me into a momma-bear hug. I wipe my tears before they can fall.

Shaun sticks his head into the backroom.

"What's going on back here? The people have come again!"

He looks at Julie then me and leaves quickly.

"How's this boy, what's his name, Jake been about this mean girl, what's her name? Britt?"

"Brooke. And gratefully, Jake has been amazing. Kind. Supportive. I feel lame. He's so amazingly beautiful and just amazing in general. Most of the time I feel like he doesn't deserve a plain-Jane like me."

"Oh, you stop! Goodness child. You're intelligent, hard-working, kind, friendly, and beautiful to boot."

She hugs me again. I smile. I love this lady like a mother.

"We better get back out there. Shaun's gonna freak-out!"

We came out, and boy howdy was it busy! We all work and work until cleanup time. We get out of there by about 10:30 pm. I'd asked for Saturday off, so I let Julie and Shaun know I won't see them until Tuesday.

"Keep your chin up, sweet girl," Julie yells after me.

I smile and give her a wave goodbye. I look around quickly to make sure Brooke isn't lurking in the shadows. Nada. Phew. I jump into Old Blue and high-tail it home. Home. My safe place. Hallelujah for my sweet yellow house!

I take my time doing my bedtime routine. I need to own a few free verse lines. I'm feeling heavy in my heart.

I write in my journal:

"What's wrong with mean girls? Or mean people in general? What gives them the right to be so cruel to others? Who makes them better than others? Blondie is the worst. My heart has been squished. I feel defeated. Mean girls suck."

CHAPTER SEVENTEEN

fter washing my face and brushing my teeth. I have a convo with my favorite mirror.

"Soooo, you know I've told you about that dumb blonde girl? Brooke?" I enlighten my mirror about all of the happenings between myself and Brooke over the last little while. It always feels good to release my tense thoughts and feelings like this. I know it sounds cheesy, but it's very therapeutic!

I shoot a few texts off before I drift off to sleep.

To Jake.

To Claire.

I literally crawl into bed like a toddler. I am exhausted both physically and emotionally. I am also beyond happy that it's Saturday tomorrow. Hallelujah!

I open my eyes. Slowly. I roll over and grab my phone. 11:45 am. Bless. Up. I need this day off. I'm worn out. School, work, homework, but most of all the emotional roller coaster I've been on with Brooke has left me feeling so upset and sad and then happy with Jake. I mean, who can keep up with these ups and downs? Sheesh! I check my phone again. Two texts from Jake.

'Hey, sleepy head, r u awake yet?'

And:

'Hey, text me when you're up!'

So, I answer. 'I'm awake! What's up?'

'There she is. Was thinking we could take Beth and Meg out today with us. What do you think?'

'Great idea. What time?'

'Meg said she and Beth have some school stuff to do, then about three pm they'll be free. I can swing over and get you all.'

'Sounds fabulous.'

I can leisurely shower, do my wash and some homework before Jake comes to get us all. I need to check in with Mom and Zac, too.

'Mom-Beth and I were going to go with Meg and Jake around 3pm today. I can grab some pizza from Sicily's for dinner, would that work?'

'My girl! Yes, that sounds terrific. Kenneth and I are going out later tonight, but Zac and Sarah will be around.'

'Awesome-luv u.'

'Luv u Gracie.'

After I shower and while I'm dressing, I call Clara. It's been a hot minute since we've hung out. Lately she's been dating this great guy named Jaxon, so we've been able to just check in with each other here and there. Grateful for our friendship and that we can stay close and not always see each other. Sign of a legit friend in my book.

"It's 2:30pm! Suhweet! I have time to fold my clothes and then Jake will be here. I need to make sure Meg and Beth will be done in time," I tell my large mirror in my room. For the most part, I enjoy conversing with my bathroom mirror, but lately, I've been working on my outfit-game, so the full-length mirror is winning the conversion game!

'Yo, chicka, will you and Meg be done in 30 min?'

'Yes. We're actually done and we are getting ready.'

'Cool thx.'

I finish folding and putting away my clothes. I do a once-over check of my outfit and pack up my purse full of things I'll need for the day.

'Here! You lovely girls ready to go?'

'Yes! We're coming!'

Jake texts me from his Jeep when he's in our driveway. I'm glad for our plan to all hang out for the afternoon. We hit the Stonebriar Mall. It's two floors, so we usually start on the bottom level. I mean, I know I've come here a thousand times, but to hold hands with Jake while perusing the mall is like top of my list of some of my happiest things I didn't even know I needed to do in my life!

We make it to the food court, and gratefully, there's a lull in the crowds of people lining up to get some of the many delicious food choices here. We all decide on Chick-fil-A. I save a table after we've all ordered. Meg and Beth help Jake bring our order to the tables. I snatch two tables, since there are four of us. We're happily eating and talking and laughing together, when I pause mid-bite.

There is NOOOOOO WAYYYY. I smell her perfume before I see her walking up to us with Justin in tow, looking like a lovesick puppy.

"Well, hello everyone," Brooke coos.

"Hey guys," we all say in a discombobulated manner.

"How come you didn't text us to tell us to meet you here?" Brooke whimpers as she says this.

I am about to say something when Jake starts to speak.

"Grace and I wanted to take our sisters out together today. It's been our plan for a few weeks now."

"Oh, well sure. That's cool. Whatever. Well, we've gotta go. *Come on,* Justin."

Brooke is so rude to Justin and demanding. I've given up on him anyway. He's doing his own thing these days, and it involves Brooke, so I'm out with Justin. Like I've hardly even spoken three words to him for weeks. But, since he's picked Brooke over me and Clara, then I don't have any desire to be his friend anymore.

And they're gone. We all look at each other and shrug. I do give Jake a super big grin and whisper, "Thank you." Not like I couldn't have handled it. But, it was nice to NOT have to handle her today, 'ya know?

We make a few more stops after the mall. One being Sicily's Pizza and Handel's ice cream. I text home to see if Zac is around or Mom to turn on the oven. Everyone is actually home! It's a Christmas miracle! So, it's going to be a big pizza and ice cream shindig together! Sweet.

We drive home with all the goods, while jamming to sweet tunes together. What a great day! I sigh with contentment. I turn my head to look at Jake, just as he happened to look at me. We both smile and tighten our grip on each other's hands.

Jake pulls into the driveway. He comes around and lets us all out. So sweet. Really. The girls grab the shopping bags. I've got the ice cream, and Jake handles all of the pizzas!

The oven is already on so when we've all said our hellos and hugged it out, Jake and I start to bake the pizzas together in the kitchen. I take out each pizza after it's cooked, and Jake slices them up. Zac and Sarah set the table and fill the drinking glasses with ice. Meg and Beth help mom make a salad, and in about forty-five minutes, we are all seated.

Mom calls on Zac to bless the dinner. "Amen!" we all say in unison.

I hungrily grab two large pieces of the veggie with white sauce pizza—my fave—and I stuff a good-sized bite into my mouth. Surprising how pizza can lift your spirits almost immediately. Jake begins to prattle on about our day at the mall with me, Beth, and his sister. The conversation turns to Kenneth and how things are going at his publishing company and then Mom gives us a good update about her book, and Zac and Sarah update us on their college applications and ACT scores. They've got a few more apps to fill out then fingers crossed they get into Steven F. Austin College!

Then, Jake shares some details about his mom. I see Meg squirm a bit. Jake continues, "Umm, so my mom is working on coming home. Well, coming back to our home. Here" We are all silent. "Dad has been talking to her—a lot—and he's told us he feels she's on the level and that she's sincere in her regret for leaving. She knows it was selfish and that she shouldn't have left us all." We all mutter our happiness at her hopefully coming home sooner than later.

Then Jake changes the subject to his dad's job and the traveling he is going to have to be doing. Jake looks at me. He tries to keep the mood light. It has been a heck of a week for me as well as for Jake. I forgot to mention this in my journal. I'll do it tonight. The situation with his mom is putting a lot of strain on their family.

Fortunately, or unfortunately, Beth takes a drink of her water and swallows it down the wrong side in her throat. Well, it's enough to break up the tense mood and we all start laughing hysterically.

Dinner conversation resumes after the laughing, and as each person finishes, they clear their spot and put their plates and cups in the dishwasher. I'm on dish duty today and tomorrow, so I thank everyone for helping a girl out!

I timidly peek at my phone I left on the kitchen counter, afraid of what I might see! Thankfully, I have zero hate-texts from Brooke. I'm sure hoping it's because I chewed her out on Friday and also because Jake spoke up at the mall today. Thank goodness.

Mom suddenly speaks up after we've all cleaned and are gathered in the family room.

"Jake, I've been thinking. Megan is more than welcome to stay with us when your father travels. It would be no trouble at all and as we all know, Beth and Meg love each other!"

"Oh, that would be marvelous. Really. Let me talk with my dad. Since, obviously, my mom isn't around yet, that would be super helpful. I'm not so good at the mom thing." He doesn't elaborate. I laugh and look at him and smile warmly.

"And you must come for dinner every night. We take turns around here, so we can just add you and Meg to the rotation, if you are comfortable with that."

"Great! I am so good at cooking any and all frozen products that are microwavable!"

We all laugh! I could feel any tension drain out of us all. Family. Want an amazing thing it is to have a fantastic family. We laugh and laugh so hard at all of the hilarious stories we end up sharing all together. It's just what everyone needed!

"Mrs. Miller, think I can take Gracie for a quick walk?"

"Jake, please just call me Ms. Kathy and yes, of course!"

I turn toward Jake and say, "That would be lovely, Jake. It is so gorgeous tonight. Thanks, Mom!"

"Of course. You kids have fun. Grab a sweatshirt though, huh?"

"Sure, Mom, and thanks for a fun evening Ms. Miller, I mean Ms. Kathy," Jake says sweetly.

CHAPTER EIGHTEEN

*J*ake gets his fave black Nike sweatshirt and I put on my baby-pink zip up sweatshirt. He opens the front door and gestures for me to follow suit. He's quiet. I'm quiet, and I enjoy this. Grabbing my hand, we walk in silence. It's actually cool this evening. Bless up for fall finally gracing us with its presence! There is a slight breeze that carries pleasant smells depicting the season.

I love Texas for its variety of smells year 'round. It's a comfort to me. It takes us about five or six minutes to reach the swings. One of our fave pastimes. But as we reach the swing set, Jake surprises me and pulls me toward him and puts his strong arms around me. I fit right under his chin. Like two interlocking puzzle pieces. Corny, I know, but a cool corny.

I can feel his warm breath on the top of my head as I rest it against his chest, which is also warm and muscular. He smells so amazingly wonderful. I let him hold me for a long time. The gentle breeze tousles our hair as we remain in this position for what seems like forever. Jake speaks softly into my hair.

"It's been a *week*, hasn't it?"

I hear the subtle sarcasm in his voice, which makes me giggle.

"You can say that again…." I state with emphasis.

Jake pulls me in closer. I have so many pent-up emotions that have welled up inside of me and boy, do I need to have them flow out of me like a river travels down a mountain side. And then the tears begin to flow—again. I sniffle.

Jake is going to think I'm a blubbering fool.

But instead, he just kisses the top of my head and caresses my back with his hand.

"Let it out, Gracie. Brooke has been really awful to you. And obviously, you deserve better. She's just jealous of you."

"Yeah, right," I mutter.

"I promise. I know her type. She plays at being high and mighty and better than everyone, but something is amiss in her life. I know it."

We both end up pulling apart simultaneously.

Is he speaking from past experience I wonder?

I mull over these thoughts. I wipe my tears away as best as I can-good grief! I'm so done crying after tonight. Ugh.

"Ready to swing?"

"Yep."

He takes my hand and leads me to the swings. The same amazing pitter-patter of my heartstrings is happening again and again every time I am with Jake. I am falling for him more and more each day, well, tumbling is more like it….

We converse back and forth with each other for almost an hour. The gentle breeze lingers, thankfully, and I watch as it musses Jake's hair each time he swings forward. We laugh. We talk. We laugh more. We talk more.

My phone chirp interrupts our glorious interaction.

'Hey, Gracie. Y'all heading back?'

I slow my swing and check my phone.

"Hey, Jake, Mom wants us to head back."

'Yep-on way home.'

"Let's go, Gracie Lou!" Jake laughs and grabs me by the hand and gently pulls me from my swing. It takes a mere ten minutes to walk to my house from our little park. We round the corner and there it is—

my cheery yellow house. I love to see it anytime I come around the corner, whether walking or driving. It warms my heart 'cause my home is my safe haven.

We get to my door; push the door open and both walk into the kitchen, where we hear a lot of voices. We've walked into a milk and cookie fest!

Jake laughs and asks, "Ready, Megs? We gotta go!"

"Yep. Just need to grab my backpack in Beth's room." Meg sprints up and down the stairs in like three minutes!

"Bye, everyone!" Meg shouts as she walks to our front door.

"Thanks everyone, especially you, Ms. Kathy, It was a great Saturday." Jake says sweetly. "Gracie," he turns his beautiful face and piercing blue eyes in my direction. "Text me when you're home from church tomorrow will 'ya?"

"Sure thing!" I smile as I say this and as I rapidly blush!

Everyone shouts goodbye, and I watch them as they pull out. I sigh a deep sigh of contentment.

"Love you guys! I'm exhausted, so I'm gonna head to bed!"

"G'night, sweetie. Boy, I sure like both Jake and Meg." Mom smiles as she says this toward me.

"Me too." I smile as I ascend the stairs-I feel like I'm floating, I'm so happy.

Sunday came and went. AND without any mean texts or drop ins from Brooke—phew! Jake and Meg came over in the afternoon and we played games, ate, watched movies and then we all did some homework. We had to buckle down somewhat to pretend like we were all four responsible students! They hung out with us until about nine pm. Then it was time for them to go.

Sighhhhh-parting IS such sweet sorrow!

And then, it's Monday. Again. But on this particular Monday, Brooke apparently is playing a new game, and she doesn't even saunter into the classroom and talk to me! Lucky me is what I say. In fact, not only does she not talk to me, she barely looks at me, like she didn't even acknowledge my presence!

I mean I guess that's fine, but it is a little uncomfortable, especially whenever I walk by her chatting in a group of people. Per usual, they start to laugh at whatever Brooke has just said, and all I can figure is they were talking about me and how I'm such a loser. Sigh. Whatever.

Brooke does, of course, hang all over every word that came out of Jake's mouth. It's so vomitous. Ew. And she does try to hug and hang on Jake physically, but he wouldn't have it! YAY!

So, other than the awkward feelings I periodically feel all day long, I don't care a bit. Because I'm with Jake now and like, we are officially dating! To say that I feel like I am in heaven is an understatement!

Maybe I actually got through to Brooke the other day?

It was just a week ago when I chewed Brooke out when she appeared at my doorstep uninvited. So, maybe she's decided to choose to ignore me because of that? Happily, I ignore her right back, too, and, to the happiness of my soul, Jake and I spend as much time as we can together, in between homework, family life and our jobs.

Oh! I forgot to say that Jake got a job at the local car repair shop. He's actually really good at working with cars and he has got some serious mechanic skills.

Still from time to time, I will have stupid doubts fly into my head, discouraging me, wanting me to believe the lies coming from somewhere deep within me. Telling me that I'm not good enough, not pretty enough, on and on-it's a real live tug-o-war of emotions in my poor brain!

I know it's dumb, but! Luckily, it doesn't happen as much anymore, and when I do start to emotionally spiral, I write down all I'm feeling in my notes on my phone or in my journal I keep on my little side table by my bed. That has helped a lot! That's the technique I learned in therapy.

Sometimes, I'll even write what's bothering me or bringing me down on a single sheet of paper, then crumple it up and throw it away. Then, once I have done all of that craziness, ha ha, then I can freely think to myself that I *so* enjoy my time with Jake, and, best of all, I now know with confidence that Jake likes me. This is such a great blessing in my life! For real.

Also, I have gotten to know his dad, too, so that has been really great. Jake and I switch off at each other's houses quite a bit now, when we aren't working. Meg comes over all the time to our house, so that's been great for Beth. Oh! Jake and Meg's mom should be coming back in December, which I hope will be a good thing and not mess everything up.

So, all in all, I am feeling happy with my overall situation! Thank. Goodness! So, if I can just continue to steer clear of Brooke, then I'm golden.

Time seems to be marching on, and in my opinion, way too rapidly. Sheesh! Before I know it, it's almost November! Like, where is the time going? Work comes and goes each week. School flies by! Life with my family and Jake's family continue to mesh together—which I like a lot—and Brooke is STILL ignoring me. But, she has taken to spreading a lot of nasty rumors about me, so that's been less than ideal.

The only part of my life that seems to go by slowly is any time I spend with Jake. Bliss. His friendship alone has helped me feel confident and sure of myself, and if I have moments or times when I miss my dad, he is my rock. He is patient and lets me cry or talk about my dad whenever I need to. It's actually very cool of him. I, in turn, am trying super hard to listen to him about his mom situation—she calls him a lot—and he's left with quite a few emotions afterward. He's not all the way convinced she'll actually come back home, so that super sucks.

Thanksgiving comes and goes. It was a lovely time! Kenneth and Mom, Jake and Meg, and their dad, Peter, and Zac and Sarah—truly having all of us together was amazing. I feel like my dad has been smiling down from heaven at all of us because everyone is doing much better emotionally and mentally, and seeing us all together. I know he's happy that *we* are happy.

Over the past few months, Megan has stayed with us anytime her dad has had to go out of town. It was really kind of my mom to offer that to her, because Meg misses her own mom so much it hurts her little heart.

One night at dinner, she just broke down in tears. Mom took her into her office and talked with her for quite a while. Since that time, Meg has been real close with my mom and Beth. Meg's mom doesn't call her really, just texts a lot. I guess since Jake is older, their mom feels she can talk with Jake more about things. I say that's bunk, but whatever. Megan is hanging in and that's all that counts.

We all make it through finals! Hallelujah! I am so stoked to be done for three weeks! Ahhh! So stoked. Christmas is in a week and a half. Jake and I and the girls have gone Christmas shopping each weekend, so we're about finished. It's one of my things to make Christmas less about getting gifts for me—buy them early and get that out of the way and then enjoy time together with family and friends.

BROOKE UPDATE: Brooke ignored me for quite some time, but then just this month (December) she went back to total mean girl crap, and when I say that I'm saying awful, mean, horrible digging comments and all. It's been the literal worst.

I've had to go back to see my therapist every week this month. My emotions and self-confidence just can't hack it. Jake has even tried to talk with Brooke, but she's been unyielding. This is another reason why I am so happy to be out of school. I never knew having a mean girl in my life could be so treacherous. I continue to thank my lucky stars that Jake and Megan moved here. Thank Goodness! Oh! And Brooke just uses Justin so badly it makes me sick, but like I said before, I can't help him when he lets her walk over him. It's ugly. I hate it. It makes me so grumps.

(FYI—Clara and I keep up via texting by the way. She and her boyfriend, Jax, are going strong and are super cute together. Makes my heart happy for her.)

Did I mention that I love winters in Texas, because they are realistically more like extended falls? Cool, some rain, maybe some ice, but most of all, very even temperatures. And right now, our weather is a balmy seventy-six degrees.

We will have a big shindig for Christmas Eve at our house: Jake, his dad Peter, and Megs, will be joining us next week for Christmas Eve. Zac and Sarah, too, obvi. And then there's the biggest news ever:

Kenneth took Zac, Beth, and me aside a few Sundays ago and asked if we would be okay if he asked Mom to marry him! We all freaked out completely and we are so happy for them both. He's going to propose on CHRISTMAS EVE! So fabulous!

Also, I need to say that Sarah and Zac are always adorable together, too, and they have already applied to multiple colleges and hopefully will be attending the same college in the fall! Wouldn't that be amazing?!

CHAPTER NINETEEN

I am brushing my teeth when I get a text.

It's from Brooke!

Oh, please no!

'Hope you enjoy Christmas, boy-stealer!'

I ignore her as always. She's like a broken record. It's not like Jake was ever into her, nor has ever been. Now she's just making a fool of herself. Also, she's supposedly dating Justin now, so why the heck is she still so obsessed with Jake? I don't get it.

Jake says it's because she's jealous because I am dating Jake and she can't handle losing out to anyone! She's such a princess. Ew. I push this crapiness out of my brain and continue to get ready. We've got a lot to do to get ready for tonight!

Mom, Zac, Beth, and I all meet up in the kitchen to divide and conquer. But before we start, we go over to Dad's memory wall and have a few moments of silence together. I will always miss my dad. He'll always be in my thoughts and heart. But over the last six months with Jake in my life, and Kenneth in my mom's life, Sarah in Zac's life, and Megan's friendship with Beth, it has turned our family right 'round to a new direction of goodness, love, and happiness.

This Christmas will be the fourth one without Dad. I do feel that time passing has helped heal my hurting heart. And Beth, Zac, and Mom, too. I have been told this many, many times, but for some reason, some days I just want to hold on to my grieving, like it will keep the memory of my dad alive in me, if I grieve. But I am slowly letting the healing power of time wash over me though and slough off the sadness, the emptiness, and loneliness. Even still, sometimes I hug his picture and cry like a child who's fallen from her bike.

MORE JAKE UPDATES: Jake has been very careful to not kiss me for a while. I am okay with this. I can love him just by looking at him or being by him, so anything he does is great, large or small. BUT Jake and I finally kissed the week of Thanksgiving. Not gonna lie. Best. Thing. Ever. We are trying to keep the kissing pretty chill, but sometimes… wow.

We have had some seriously intense make-out sessions! Anyways, things just keep moving forward. Jake's dad, Peter, loves Katy, Texas, so they're def looking for a house to buy now. Stoked for this to happen.

Peter is super nice! I mean I'm not surprised 'cause both Megan and Jake are exactly the same way—kind and nice! Oh, and their mom —Penelope—she's going to move to Katy, too! It seems that she and Peter have been working things out together, so that's very awesome. They'd only been separated for about a year, not divorced, so that is also a plus. She has fully committed to coming in January. Both Jake and Megan feel a great relief. It's been very stressful with their mom gone.

I need to mention that I have been in therapy for the first three years after Dad died. It is more than helpful. It really is. But this past year, and after nearly four years that Dad has been gone, I feel I can handle my teeter tottering emotions better, or as much as I can in my situation. So, I finished that up just before I met Jake.

Sometimes, I think back to our group sessions. In fact, I remember this one girl in our group. She was younger than me. She had lost her dad too and had been coming for two years by the time I joined. She had shared that time was the key for her. The farther she moved away from that tragic day, the better. In the first few months, she thought she'd never be able to make it to the next day. She said every day she'd look in the mirror and say, "Would Dad want me to be sad or happy? Would he want me to remember the good times, or only the day he died? Time will mend your broken heart."

Those words have stuck with me, and I can finally say that I agree with her. Time DOES mend a broken heart. Mine is not all put together, but it is getting there. Each day I arise and greet my day with happiness and good memories of my daddy, his picture is on my bedside table, and then I have the strength to move forward.

Now, as I said previously, I've been back to see my therapist since Brooke has been lashing out at me! It's helped tons. I write tons in my journal and on single sheets of paper, and I'm doing a lot of paper crumpling!

I'd like to say that I still consider Jake part of my "therapy" too. Jake and I are good for each other. Having both experienced a loss of a parent—his mom leaving, and my dad passing—has automatically bonded us together. We speak of it often together. He is still mending emotionally since his mother's departure has been more recent than my dad's death. But, since she and his dad have been working on getting back together, it is good we are able to talk together—a lot— and get some of our emotions out. I guess that's why we got along so well.

Oh! Brooke had tried the cold-shouldering to Jake, too, which didn't faze him one bit, clearly, as he won't play any childish games. He was relieved like I was. He didn't like the way she had treated me this whole time, even the ignoring, and now back to the mean girl crappola.

He gets upset about this and keeps offering suggestions of things I can say to her or things I can do or could say, but I feel content with the one time I told her off, so I keep telling him it's fine. She isn't worth my time. For real.

Actually, Brooke's behavior didn't surprise me one tiny bit 'cause she's all about herself, not anyone else, and she's all about serving her needs. She loves her hair, her clothes, her body and makes sure that she flaunts every part of herself to everyone—shocker. I mean, does she even have a nice bone in her body? Or any thoughts in her brain?

Sigh, I wish I wasn't right. I would have liked it so much better if she turned out to be actually nice, genuinely nice, but as all films and books depict, clone type girls are just that—clones like those plastic dolls. It's sad, really.

I am constantly relieved to be just normal little ol' me—mid on the hotness scale of life, ha ha, which makes me totally content. It really is a relief. I don't want to have to worry about my looks all the time. I like to study and learn and enjoy my school, work, family and Jake! I was able to handle Brooke just fine since she'd been ignoring me—thankfully—but now, the mean things she says, oh, they hurt me so badly. I just hate it so much.

"Gracie? You okay?"

"Good, good. Sorry Mom!" I jump right back into helping and quickly change the subject!

"What's left to finish, guys?"

"Just a few more food items to prepare. Gracie, if you can finish the fruit salad and green salad, then Zac and Beth will finalize the table settings. I am finishing a little more lights and decor in the family room! Oh! Someone change the music for me to the Harry Connick Jr. Christmas album, please?"

Beth yells from the family room, "Got it Mom!"

Music is on. Food is all set out. We are all dressed up and awaiting our guests. When the doorbell rings, it's Kenneth.

"Merry Christmas, everyone! Wow! You guys have outdone yourselves! The house is gorgeous." We all smile, and blush slightly, as Kenneth plants a huge kiss on Mom's lips! "Shall I put the gifts under the tree?"

"Please do sweetheart," my mom answers sweetly.

The bell rings and Zac answers it. It's Sarah. She's dressed in the most adorable velvet little black dress! She is bearing gifts also!

"Come on in Sarah!" Zac says. They too hug and kiss. Boy! So much love, ha ha. Zac directs her into the family room where Kenneth is putting his packages under the tree. She follows suit.

The doorbell rings again! And you won't believe it! It's not just Jake, Megs, and Peter, but their mom/wife is here, too. They all look amazingly happy!

"Grace, this is my mom, Penelope. Mom, this is my Grace. I mean my girlfriend, Grace!" Everyone bursts out laughing, Jake reddens, but he's still smiling.

I put out my hand to shake hers, but instead of shaking my hand, she takes it and envelops me into a huge hug.

"Grace, thank you for being so amazing to both Jake and Megan. I can't thank you enough."

"My pleasure. They're both wonderful humans."

I escort Jake and his family into the family room, too. As they all walk over toward the couches and seat themselves, I take a moment and look around at all of these amazing people and soak it all in. Lots of changes have occurred over the past four years since dad died. Changes for the better, though. Thankfully.

Jake calls my name, and I walk over to him and take my place next to him. Mom and Penelope are looking already like they'll become fast friends—not surprising knowing my mom. Everyone is chatting and laughing when Kenneth rises and calls us all to attention.

"Before the evening gets underway, I'd like to give the first gift of Christmas to Kathy." Kenneth motions for Mom to come and stand by him. He takes a little green velvet box out of his pocket and takes her hands. We are all dead silent, but for sure ready to celebrate as soon as he pops the question!

Kenneth turns toward Mom. She swallows in apprehension but is grinning ear to ear.

"Sweet Kathy, you know how much I love you and because of this, I would like to ask you to be my wife!"

"Yes!" Mom squeals out and lets Kenneth put the ring on her finger.

Needless to say, we all jump up and shout with happiness! Then we three kids crowd in for a big group hug.

"Best Christmas gift ever!" my mom shouts! Her eyes are glistening as she is admiring her ring. It is gorgeous! A huge diamond on a simple white gold band.

"Sooooo, when is the wedding date going to be?" I couldn't resist asking!

"We're thinking next summer when y'all are out of school, and that we make it a destination wedding to… Hawaii! Just all of us here. Small, but perfect with all of our loved ones." Kenneth shared this fabulous idea with us all.

"What?" Zac and Beth and I all shout in unison!

"Oh, my stars! I can hardly wait!" Beth exclaims.

"Me neither!" I say.

"We're thinking the week after school gets out in May, and Zac and Sarah graduate.

"It sounds perfect," Penelope says sweetly.

She's been very kind and sociable thus far. I'm glad she's fitting in with all of us. Jake told me a bit ago that his mom made sure she communicated daily with Peter and her kids, and also, she just stayed with her parents in Cali this past year, so that made it a bit less painful knowing she hadn't been out dating or galavanting. She just took some time off to really think.

The game changer was when Peter was told he could stay in Texas and not have to move around anymore. But that just barely happened and with that news, Penelope packed her bags and came back to her family—very humbled and apologetic.

CHAPTER TWENTY

The evening continues wonderfully. We all exchange our gifts to one another, eat so much yummy food, and read from Luke 2 and sang carols. The festivities ended just before midnight. For Christmas Day, we would all have our own separate family Christmas mornings, then meet up later on.

The rest of Christmas break passes more rapidly than I care for, and school will start on Monday—ugh. Brooke is gone all of break (Justin texted to tell me that he was sad and lonely that's how I knew, 'cause I sure didn't care) so no mean texts and stop bys. Bless up!

"Well, she glared at me today and told me I looked so blah, when you were out of earshot, and then she went about showing off her new Italian clothes she got in Italy over Christmas break to anyone and everyone all day long! I wish she'd go back to just ignoring me. I like that way better." We are in Latin and I'm filling Jake in on the daily-mean-girl updates.

"She's just trying to get a rise out of you. You're doing well to continue to blow her off, like you have been doing. This behavior is all on her and realistically, she is missing out on having you as a friend. Of course, I don't really know if you could be friends ever."

"True. We don't quite see eye to eye." I laugh very sarcastically!

We've been back in school after Christmas break for a few weeks, and from time to time we've discussed the Brooke sitch, as we call it, like today. We are both laughing and holding hands as we walk to Jake's car. He had taken to getting me before school and taking me home on days I didn't have to work right after school. I love driving with him so much. It makes me really happy.

Brooke finds a way every single day to say a mean comment to me —like *every single day*! I wish she'd just give up already.

January and February bring a lot of choir events for me. We have a thing called UIL that is a singing competition. We've been practicing every day in class and our performance will be just before Spring Break in March.

Jake says that Megan isn't too happy with her mom. She's been back for a few months now, but Megan didn't have the best rapport to begin with before her mom left for a year. Plus, she's still pretty young. Jake being older is much more emotionally mature.

We both are saying that it's been pretty cool to have our sisters become friends, and Jake has been reiterating how good it's been for Meg to have Beth—and I said ditto—they have both been so helpful to one another.

"Beth has been Meg's saving grace, to be honest,"

"I am so glad!" I happily chime in. "As has Meg for Beth. Who knew this would all work out like this when y'all moved here?"

"For real!" We are at his house with Beth and Megan, doing a fun Latin project together.

"Yeah. What a cool thing, right? I'm with my best girl and our sisters are BFFs or whatever girls say." He looks at me and I roll my eyes, laughing.

Spring break comes and goes. Jake and I cranked up our work, though, and then hung out at night so we could earn and save our money for college. At least we have one more year of school before college is even an issue. I am glad it was mellow. Even the weather was nice. And, praise be, Brooke traveled again. So, I was spared again from her being around to cause issues for me.

Our ULI competition is this week! We've prepared well for it. The only downside for me is that Brooke is in choir, too, so who knows what she'll do to me when Jake isn't around.

"Today's the day! I love UIL! And good morning to you my dear mirror!" It's been a while since I've talked to my mirror. Thinking that dating Jake has really boosted my confidence. Just sayin'. Plus, I've been using my journal way more and the write out my feelings and then crumple it up technique a lot, too. It's been working well and I'm going to therapy too.

"We got all *ones*, you guys!" I fly in the door of my cute yellow house and shout it out to whomever is there, which is mom, Zac, and Beth.

"Oh, wow! Great job!" Zac compliments.

"Fab sis, so fab," Beth chimes in.

"I always love coming to hear you sing, sweet girl," Mom sweetly shares with us all.

"Thanks guys! I appreciate your support," I grin at all of them. "I'm so tired. Heading to bed. Love y'all!" I slowly meander up the stairs. I really am so exhausted. It's the good kind of exhausted though. Then my thoughts darken, because what I didn't tell them all is how Brooke "accidentally" stomped on my makeup bag—on purpose—when we were all getting ready for our main performance.

Clara couldn't believe what she'd seen.

"I told you! She's mean to me every day!"

"That's absurd. I'm gonna go tell her off." Her brows were furrowed, and she was in attack mode. I grabbed her arm.

"Don't bother. She's not worth it. I promise I'm okay."

"Well, okay, but Grace! What's wrong with her that she thinks it's okay to treat you like that?"

"Well, I'm glad you're finally on board with me. I will say that helps me think I'm not crazy!"

"I'm sorry, Gracie. I've been in my own world, obviously, and she never ever treats me or anyone else like that, at least I don't think she does, so it was hard for me to imagine her mistreating you so badly!"

"It has to do with when she and Jake lived in the same place in California. She pursued Jake and he never reciprocated, and she just made it up that he liked her but was being coy, which is false."

"Sheesh. She's with Justin, so why doesn't she just get over it?"

"Because she doesn't like to lose."

"Oh. Ugh. I'm sorry, Grace."

Clara gave me a hug.

I will be writing this whole experience in my dang journal. Sometimes I just want to scream at the top of my lungs at Brooke. Maybe I should! I need to tell Mom, I guess. I'm feeling very over it today. I mean I've been over it for a long time actually, but today was really rough.

I drape my choir dress onto my chair, wash my face, brush my teeth, and grab my journal. It takes me thirty minutes or so to write about what Brooke did today. I didn't even tell Jake. I just didn't want to relive it again and again. At least Clara saw it firsthand today. Brooke apparently hadn't seen Clara sitting by the mirror curling her eyelashes. She thought I was alone. Well, it's about time someone sees her cruelty—even Jake doesn't see it—because she saves it for when he's not looking. I just tell him what happens to me. Sigh.

I turn out my light and lie down as the tears slowly trickle from my eyes and down my cheeks. *It's time to tell my mom, and it's time to straighten Brooke out. I can't take any more of this!*

I SNOOZE MY ALARM THREE MORE TIMES BEFORE I CAN MUSTER ENOUGH strength to roll out of bed. I cried for a long time last night. I also decided I'm going to talk to Mom this morning. I'm done. I'm so done.

I throw my hair up into a scrunchie and amble down the stairs to the kitchen.

"Morning!"

"Well, thank you for gracing us with your presence!" Zac remarks sarcastically.

"Very funny," I retort. "I was a little exhausted," I breathe out.

"Just kidding sis—I know—what's up with you today?"

"I'm actually going to ask Mom if she'd like to go to lunch with me today. Where's Beth?"

"Gone. Volleyball, then hanging with Meg."

"Ha—not surprised."

"Me neither!"

"What's up with you and Sarah?"

"We both have work this afternoon, then we will go out later. Are you seeing Jake today?"

"Yeah. I'll text him in a bit. Need to check in with Mom and see what she's got going on first, then we will make plans."

"Sounds great! Oh, I made your favorite—pancakes! I saved them on the counter for you."

"Ah, thanks bro." I give him a hug. Then, I grab the pancakes, uncover them and zap them in the microwave for a bit and smother them in syrup. I pour a cup of milk and scarf it all down in about ten minutes. While I'm eating, I text Mom.

'Hey, Mom, where are you?'

Her text pops up.

'Went to Winco quickly. Be home in five. What's up?'

'Wondering if you've got time for a lunch date with me today.'

'I'd love that. How about in an hour? Then we can both get ready.'

'Perf. See you soon.'

I dress as quickly as I can. I'm so anxious about all of this with Brooke. I want to get it off of my chest. I'm feeling very stressed about it now and since I've resolved to tell my mom, I just want to get it over with! I send Jake a text.

'Going to lunch with my mom. Meet up later?'

'Oh fun-of course-I'm off at 5 tonight. How about I come over?'

'Excellent c u later.'

I descend the stairs to call for Mom.

"Ma, ready?"

"I'm here Gracie." In her office. I enter and see she's just finishing and emailing.

"Sent! I've got some news for you. I just found out that my books have been picked up by Dando productions to make The Sunflower Children from the Underworld series into movies! I need to finish book eight, but I have the basic layout, etc. Can you even believe this?"

I'm so stunned I don't even know what to say! "Mommm!" I scream! "You did it! I'm so freaking proud of you!" We embrace in a warm hug. "Holy, Mom, I'm so happy for you!"

"It's all because of Kenneth. He's been so encouraging to me, especially when your dad died, he helped me to dive into my writing even more, and boy, did it pay off!"

"Yeah, it did!"

We walk out of her office and to the front door.

"I'll drive us today," Mom states, giggling.

"Very funny. I know how you feel about Old Blue." I roll my eyes at her and we climb into her Lexus. She recently got a new car from the proceeds of book seven.

"I'm going to buy you a new car before your senior year, sweetie."

"What? Mom for real?"

"Yep, it's time to get rid of Old Blue."

"Uh, no argument here!"

We decide to eat at Mi Cocina. It's about fifteen minutes from our house. Saturday lunch times aren't nearly as crowded as dinner time, so we get a table almost immediately.

"Well, this is nice. We haven't done this for months! And I apologize."

"Mom, please don't apologize. I'm just as busy, and when I'm not doing something, I'm with Jake."

"Okay, true. But, still, this *is* nice."

"It truly is."

We order our food, and then I begin.

"So, I've been needing to talk with you about something I should have shared with you earlier. I don't know why I haven't. Anyways. It's Brooke. Ever since I started hanging with Jake, Brooke has been so mean to me.

"What? For this long? And you're just telling me now?"

"I know, I know. I'm sorry." The tears gather in my eyes.

"Oh, sweetie, don't cry."

"Oh, Mom! It's been just awful. Jake has tried to talk with her—she just ignored him—then I told her off last semester. Then she went to ignoring me, or being mean to me when no one can see, and never in front of Jake. Yesterday, she stomped on my makeup bag but guess what? Clara was on the floor doing her makeup when Brooke comes by and literally with all of her weight stomped on my makeup bag! Clara gasped and Brooke just said, "Oops!" and walked away!"

"You've got to be kidding me!"

"Nope! Truth."

"Oh, you poor girl," she puts her hand on mine. I let it stay there until our food comes. We eat and I divulge all of the horrid things that have happened over the past eight months!

"Gracie, why didn't you tell any of us? We are your family!"

"Because I thought Jake and I could handle it well, now just me, because Brooke does mean things sneakily—but for some reason, yesterday was too much and I snapped this morning. I mean, I know I've gained so much confidence dating Jake, and he has helped me see who I am and he has given me the courage to be stronger and confident because HE believes that I am a great person. And he tells me this often, and now I believe it! But this stuff with Brooke is killing me and it's making me crazy. I'm going to confront her and tell her to leave me alone."

"I think you have no other choice."

"What if she still keeps it up?"

"Then you keep telling her to leave you alone and loud and in front of others so you can get their support."

"Okay, true. That's a good idea."

"I wish I could do it for you, but I know I can't. And boy, I hate this for you."

We eat and chat for another hour. This lunch is therapy in and of itself for me!

CHAPTER TWENTY-ONE

*J*ake rings the bell.

"Come in!" I yell from the kitchen. I know it's him because he just texted me, ha ha.

"Hey you!" He enters the kitchen and wraps me in a warm hug, then kisses me. Sigh. Nothing better than that for me.

"You smell so fresh and clean!"

"Just showered. Was a sweaty, dirty mess before," he laughs and smiles at me, which in turn lights up his amazing blue eyes.

"Well, in that case, I thank you! I made us some dinner, are you hungry?"

"Starved!"

"Excellent. Come on and sit. I'll dish us up. I think Beth and Meg are heading back over here soon, right?"

"Yeah, my mom will drop them off."

"Cool, maybe we can all watch a movie together?"

"Oh, that sounds excellent. I'm beat."

"Me too! And I need to tell you a few things…." I began.

"Yes? What's up?"

"Yesterday at the choir UIL, Brooke "accidentally" stomped on my makeup bag. Well, Clara saw and was flabbergasted."

"Accidentally? Please. Everything she does to you is well thought-out and definitely premeditated."

"Oh, I'm aware! Anyways, I finally told my mom—everything. She wasn't real happy I kept everything from her. Oh yeah, I didn't tell you that I never told her anything cause I thought we could handle it —or I could—but yesterday was the last straw."

"Uh, I would have done that months ago. You're a better person than I am."

"No, I'm not. I'm actually dumb because I just can't believe I've allowed this to go on for soooooo long. Anyways, Monday I'm ready to confront her head on, loudly, and in front of everyone."

Jake pulls me in for a warm hug—sigh—my heart melts every time he comes near me!

In my ear he whispers, "You are an amazing, kind, and awesome person. You can do this with Brooke."

He leans back a bit and kisses my cheek and then we snuggle as I put on *The Grinch* with Jim Carey and chill together until Megan and Beth show up around an hour later.

"Hello! We're here!" Beth speaks this loudly as she enters the house. Megan follows her in.

I state happily, "Hey cuties! Come and join us."

"Y'all have popcorn?" Megan inquires.

"Nah, forgot to pop it," Jake says wearily. "But if you're up tonight sis, go for it!"

"Sure, Jake sure," Megan says sarcastically but is still smiling.

Mom and Kenneth are out but are to be coming home soon. Jake and I are only going to stay up until around ten-ish. We are both too tired, ha ha.

Popcorn popped and even lemonade to drink, all on a cute tray that Megan and Beth bring in together.

"Thanks, girls!" Jake and I both gush out happily. "Seriously. We had zero energy!" I say.

We all finish *The Grinch* and then Beth puts on *Christmas Vacation*. We laugh and laugh. It's such a ridiculously funny movie!

"Sorry to bail girls, but Megan and I need to head home."

"We understand," both Beth and I chirp.

"I'm headed to bed, too," I say tiredly.

"Me too!" Beth says.

I walk out with Jake to his Jeep. He's let Megan in already. We hug and kiss goodnight.

"Sleep well, sweet Grace," Jake takes my hand and squeezes it.

"You too, my handsome Jake. You too." He holds my hand, and I walk and slowly slip my hand out as I walk backward to the door. I wave as he pulls out.

Be still my heart.

Sunday—it's two am and my phone beeps—I see this later. But I didn't wake to that. Instead, I'm awakened by my cell ringing.

"What? What are you saying, Justin!" I feel panicky. My hands are sweating.

"It's Brooke. She-she's been in a bad car accident, Grace. She's at Baylor. I-I need you, Grace. Please." Justin is sobbing now.

"Okay, listen. Let me get dressed. I need to tell my mom. And I'll be there. Do you want me to tell Jake?"

"Yes. Yes. Please. Both of you come. Please…." His voice drops off and he hangs up. It's only then that I see another text.

Oh, my gosh. It's from Brooke at 1:30 am! That was just like thirty min ago. What in the world?

'I am sorry Gra—'

And it cuts off. Holy.

She must have crashed just barely after she tried to send this message.

I throw on my clothes from yesterday that are in a pile on my floor. I call Jake.

"Hello? Grace? What's wrong?" He sounds panicky.

"I'm fine. It's, umm, it's Brooke. She's been in a horrible accident. Justin just called me like five minutes ago. And he's like us to come down to Baylor. Can you come?" I feel tears kick my very tired eyes.

"Of course. Let me talk with my parents. I'll text when I'm in your driveway." He hangs up.

I scurry down the hall and knock on Mom's door and open it slowly. I don't want to scare her to death.

"Mom? Mom, it's Grace."

She bolts up. "What is it, sweetie? Are you okay?" She sounds terrified. Ugh. I tried to not have her feel this way. Oh, well.

"I'm fine. But-but Justin called," I'm crying now. Although in the back of my mind some stray thoughts are niggling my mind.

What is my brain trying to tell me?

"It's Brooke. She's been in a terrible accident. Justin wants Jake and I to come and be with him." I frown. This is a lot. I'm getting scared vibes like when my dad died.

No. Not again.

"What? What in the world! Oh, my goodness. Okay, okay. So is Jake coming?" She still sounds panicky.

"Yes. He's probably almost here. I packed up a bag of snacks and a book and my phone charger. I'll text when I know more. Oh! I almost forgot. Mom. Brooke sent me a half-written text."

I show her my phone.

"Oh, Grace."

"Yeah. I know."

She hugs me and kisses the top of my head. "Be well, my precious. You're a good friend."

I blow her a kiss and quietly close her door in the hopes that she can get back to sleep quickly.

Why are you going, Grace? What has Brooke ever done for you? Why would you go and help Justin? He's been lame and a very bad friend.

I stop mid-stairs.

Why am I going? Because. Justin and I have been friends forever. I'm doing this for him. Not for her.

I feel resolved enough with these few thoughts—I think.

My phone chirps.

Jake.

'Here.'

I run out, closing the door as softly as I can and dash 'round to the passenger side (a few months ago I told Jake that he's the best and most chivalrous, ha ha, but that I'm just fine to get in and out of the car myself!)

"Hi."

"Hey."

"Thanks, Jake."

He grabs my hand. He's always warm. I love that about him. He smiles at me, and we fall into comfortable silence. The hospital is about fifteen minutes away. Jake doesn't even put on any music.

"I'm doing this for Justin," I say flatly.

"Ditto. And for you." He smiles warmly at me again.

Pitter-patter. My heart is always doing this when I'm with Jake.

"I had a moment at home where I just didn't know if I could come. But as you know, Justin and I have been friends for years," I explain.

"Sure, sure. And I wouldn't blame you one bit."

"And to think on Monday I was going to confront her. Wow."

"I know, Grace. I literally just thought of that. Right now."

"Yeah. Weird. Not even karma. What do you call this. Super bad luck?"

He shrugs. I shrug.

C'est la vie!

Jake pulls into a parking spot. It's obviously very empty this time of the morning. We get out and he clicks the key fob to lock his Jeep. The beep echoes cause it's so empty! Being April, the weather is lovely, but we both are in sweatshirts anyways because hospitals can be chilly.

The automatic doors open slowly, and we walk through them. I feel sort of like this isn't happening, like and out of body experience or like I'm watching this all take place in a movie!

I speak up as we reach the front desk.

"Hi. We're wanting to go to Brooke Marchant's room, please."

"Okay, let me check where she is at." The nice lady is scrolling on her laptop.

"Looks like she's in surgery. You're welcome to wait on the med-surge third floor waiting room."

"K. Thanks."

We traverse the hallway to the elevators. I text Justin.

'Hey. Jake and I are coming to the third floor waiting room. The front desk lady says Brooke is in surgery?'

'Yeah. She broke her left arm and right leg. She's got gashes all over her and she hit her head—hard. She-she's a mess. I'll fill you both in when you get up here.'

I have Jake read Justin's text while we ride the elevator up.

"Oh, that sucks. Poor Brooke."

"For real. That's so many injuries! Sheesh."

As we step off the elevator, Justin is waiting for us. I pull him into a long hug. He cries. He's really tall, so his tears wet by hair. He pulls away and wipes his face. He reaches out to shake Jake's hand, but Jake gives him a big bear hug instead.

"I can't thank you guys enough for coming down."

"Of course, Justin," we both say. "Friends support friends."

"Well, I've been a super crappy friend for a long while, so I extra appreciate you both." He finished his sentence really in a super quiet voice. I grab his hand.

"Let it go. We're friend always no matter what. Okay?" I tell him.

"Okay.

"Did you find out what happened?" I question.

"Yeah. She'd had a fight with her dad and went out driving—fast, apparently—and crashed at The Bend."

"Oh, crap."

"Yeah. Oh, crap is right."

"Uh, guys, what's The Bend?" Jake queries.

Justin answers with intended melancholy. "The Bend is a really curvy downhill road that has a lot of scary turns. So many accidents have happened there due to people's high speeds."

I chime in. "Yeah. She probably didn't know how curvy it was, I don't know."

He continued. "Not sure if she's ever driven it. I mean, she's never shared that info with me. We'd gone out early last night. I'd dropped her home by midnight, so obviously something happened when she got home with her dad, because an hour or so later she texted me saying that she'd had a fight with her dad and asked if she could come over and talk, but she never arrived."

"What!? Oh Justin. I'm so, so sorry."

"Yeah. Brooke's dad calls me shortly after she'd texted me. I told him she should have been here by now. He said he was going out looking for her, so he hung up but then called him right back cause he'd received the news from the cops." Justin finishes his story and huffs. Poor kid. He's worried. He's exhausted. Emotional. Ugh.

My heart hurts for him. I knew that if the situation was switched and it was Jake in surgery right now, I'd be absolutely devastated.

"Oh, I just can't believe it. This is so awful. She's so young to have all this happen to her," I say to Justin and Jake.

"I know. Her dad and mom are back in the surgery waiting room. They'll come tell us when she's out." Justin sighs a deep sigh. He's sitting between Jake and me. We all sigh and just sit back and say nothing. Time is moving really slowly. And all my brain can think of is, *why did this happen? How did this happen? And to Brooke? I mean, she's the perfect one like a perfect plastic doll. She can't be broken or hurt, can she?*

We sit quietly for what feels like forever but ends up being about two hours. We've all closed our eyes for a bit, too. Suddenly, we hear footsteps, and we all jolt awake.

"Mr. Marchant. This is Jake and Grace. Friends of Brooke and I. Is she out of surgery?"

His facial expression is so grim.

"She is but she's slipped into a coma." He frowns.

We are all frozen. What do you say to that?

CHAPTER TWENTY-TWO

"Oh, I'm so sorry sir." Justin is such a good boy.

"I know you are, son. You all can come and see her. Be prepared. She's very, very banged up and bruised and bandaged. The surgeon said with the amount of trauma she suffered, he's not surprised that she's in a coma. It's actually a positive because her body is assessing her wounds and will work to heal them and in a coma, she can rest and and…."

He couldn't finish. Oh, my heart! Tears well in my eyes again. I know I don't care how mean she has been to me. This is her dad. This is his little girl.

He turns abruptly and motions for us to follow him to the elevator. We follow like little sheep following a sheep hound. No one utters a word. The ride upstairs is dead silent. The elevator dings and we continue to follow Mr. Marchant. We are in the fourth floor—ICU. As we near her room, I see Mrs. Marchant holding Brooke's right hand since her other arm is in a cast. As we get nearer, I turn and look at Brooke.

Holy crap. Holy, holy crap.

Her hair is mussed. There's blood all in it. Her left eye is swollen.

She's got bandages and casts and bruises like everywhere. I stop dead in my tracks.

I don't know if I can go in there. This is just like my dad looked after his accident. Only he died. What if she dies? No, no, no, no! She's can't. Her parents. Justin. Nooooo.

Jake arrives at my side.

"You okay?" he whispers to me.

"Noooo. I'm not okay." I whisper back. "It's like when my dad—"

Jake grabs my hand. He holds it tightly.

"I'm sorry. Gracie. I didn't even think about this event churning up past memories. I'm sorry I wasn't thinking of that for you."

"Please don't apologize. I don't even think I told you all of the details, but yeah. She's looks as bad as he did, and he died!" I whisper this with tears falling down my cheeks.

We stand still holding hands as we watch Justin enter Brooke's room. We can't quite hear what he's saying, but he's definitely talking to her. And then wet tears start to fall from his eyes. We all just look on as this is unfolding in front of our eyes. Brooke's mom walks out to change places with her husband as he is taking his turn now with Justin.

Mrs. Marchant comes toward us.

"Thank you both for coming down to see Brooke. I know she'll be glad that her friends came to see her. Jake. It's good to see you again. It's been a while." She smiles warmly and gives us both a hug. Jake and I smile back.

"I'm going downstairs to get some food. Will you tell my husband Bruce where I went?"

"Of course, Mrs. Marchant. Of course." I squeak out.

"Oh, please call me Mary, dear. No need to be so formal."

We watch her walk around us and hear her footsteps clomp slightly toward the elevators. It's so quiet on this floor. Holy. Oh! Did I mention that she is dressed in what looks like a sweatsuit and running shoes, but that it's a fancy-shmancy sweatsuit! And she has on the dope Brooks running shoes I want. Her pretty blonde hair is pulled back in a sleek ponytail.

Like mother like daughter. Also, can I interrupt this scene to say um, Mary? If you only knew how your daughter has treated me for months and months, then you'd think that I am anything but a friend to her. Nor is Jake.

I don't share my thoughts with Jake. I just let it be.

There is a bench outside Brooke's room. Jake starts to walk forward and motions for me to follow him. We settle ourselves on the bench just as Mr. Marchant and Justin come out of Brooke's ICU room. Jake and I stand in unison and offer them both the bench. It's our turn!

Be calm Grace. You can do this. You've got this or whatever that phrase moms and dads say to their kids. I've got this. Do I?

We walk in as silently as we can. I mean, I know she can't hear us but still, I feel the need to be reverent and respectful. We both pull up the two chairs in the room to her right side. Jake looks at me and takes my hand, and his hand and puts it on Brooke's one unbruised hand. She's warm. *Well, obvi, she's not dead, Grace!*

"Hey Brooke, it's Grace and Jake. We are so sorry this happened to you. I can't believe it! We are all in shock. Just know that we will come and visit you and be praying for you to wake up." I get choked up and can't say any more, so Jake takes over.

"For sure, Brooke. We are both here for you. We hope you wake up really soon and that you heal quickly. Your parents are here, and Justin has been here since you were brought in by ambulance earlier."

Then we just sit there and tears well up in both of our eyes. We continue to hold her hand for about ten more minutes. Jake rises first and lifts me up out of my chair. We walk solemnly out of Brooke's room.

"So, hey, Justin, we're going to go home and sleep for a bit then we will come up later. Want us to go by your house and get some clothes and stuff for you?"

"That would actually be terrific. I'll head home later on. I'm gonna stay for a while longer. Let me text my mom. She can put together a bag of stuff for me. And guys? Thanks again for coming so quickly. I truly appreciate it." We all hug and we wave goodbye to Mary and

Bruce and begin our walk to the elevators. When the door shuts and Jake has pushed floor one, I let out a huge sigh.

"Ditto on that sigh—man, that was tough. How in the world did you even get through that with your dad?" He envelops me in a loving, warm hug and kisses the top of my head. I love when he does this.

And I think to myself, *how did I survive? Beth? Zac? My mom?*

"To be honest, I don't know, Jake. Much of it is a blur, and yet other parts are crystal clear and embedded into my memory forever."

"Well, I knew you were tough, but dang girl. You, your siblings, your mom, wow."

"Yeah, wow is right. They're pretty awesome."

Jake drops me home. It's almost five am. I wearily walk upstairs and fall flat onto my deliciously, amazing, queen bed. I don't even undress. I plug in my phone and am asleep before I even know it.

My phone pings.

Where am I? What's happening right now?

I grab my phone, four pm! Holy schnikes! I can barely see out of my sleepy eyes, ha ha.

"Oh, it's Jake!"

'Grace girl, you up? I just woke up!'

'Oh, my gosh, me too! I slept like a rock in a thicket of trees!'

'Me too. I'm going to shower and eat then I'll come over. Is that cool?'

'Yep-I'll do the same.

Thirty minutes later, I'm in the kitchen telling Zac, Sarah, Beth, Meg, Mom, and Kenneth the low-down on Brooke, while Mom is dishing up some leftover pasta for me and Beth is pouring me a cup of milk and buttering some bread, too.

"She's in a coma, which the doc says is actually a good way for her to heal due to all of her injuries."

"Does her car not have airbags? Why was she so hurt?" This is Beth asking the question.

"Yeah, I texted Justin right when I woke up and asked that very same question. I guess she was so upset that she forgot to put on her seatbelt."

Zac groans. "Oh dude. Poor girl."

Sarah adds, "What is her prognosis?"

"She should come out of it in a few weeks, so let's hope this will actually happen."

Megan sighs. "What a bummer. I am so sorry for her. Did anyone mention the fight with her dad?"

"No. Not at all. I was afraid to even ask Justin, 'cause I am sure her dad feels super guilty as it is." Everyone nods their heads in agreement.

Kenneth chimes in, "I am truly sorry for their family. Why don't we buy some food cards for her parents, and you and Jake can take them up with you when you go?"

"Great idea, Kenneth." My mom brushes his cheek and smiles.

"Come and eat, Grace," Beth declares firmly. "You must be famished!"

I sit down at the table and scarf the food down.

"Dang, this is sooo good!"

"Glad you like it, sweetie."

We hear a quiet knock at the door and Jake pops his head in. "Hello?"

Kenneth calls to him, "We are all in the kitchen, Jake, come on through."

Jake's hair is still wet. Holy. He looks good with mussed hair, wet hair, and in anything he wears. Dang, he's gorgeous. If I was a cartoon character, I'd have hearts over my eyes right now! He steps softly to the table, pulls out a chair, and plops down beside me.

"Hi."

"Hi back."

"You smell amazing!"

"You look adorable." I blush.

"Hey, Jake, we were all talking and came up with the idea to put our funds together to get some food cards for the Marchants. Would you and Grace mind hitting Costco before heading up to the hospital?" Zac asks Jake.

"Yeah, no problem. Should we grab flowers?"

Mom says, "Sure. Even if Brooke isn't awake, it will brighten the room for her parents. Good idea."

A Venmo-palooza breaks out and Jake and I are ready to go.

"Thanks, everyone. This is really great of you guys. And, even though, you know there's been bad blood between Brooke and me, I'm definitely not heartless enough to not care for another human being."

Mom gives me a hug and kisses my cheek.

"We wouldn't think you'd act any other way, Grace. Your heart is too good."

I blush again. "Okay, I'll text when we get to the hospital. See y'all later!"

The room explodes with raucous goodbyes and good lucks, and we exit the kitchen and then head out the front door. It takes us a good thirty minutes to pick which food cards we think they'd like, then we purchase them and some flowers and are finally on our way.

"How do you feel, Jake?"

"Pretty good, how about you?"

"Not as bad as I thought I'd feel getting such sporadic sleep."

Jake laughs and grabs my hand. He's got his Spotify playlist on. I rest my head and gaze out the window as we drive towards Baylor Hospital.

I still can't believe this happened! I hope Brooke wakes up, but most of all, I hope she'll be nice to me when she does....

I keep these thoughts to myself 'cause I just don't know how this all will come out.

Will she wake up? And if she does, then what?

"Wow. Big difference in the parking lot at 6:30 pm than two am!" I laugh because it's packed.

"Did you text Justin?"

"Yeah, I did. Forgot to tell you. He says to come up to the fourth floor again."

"Cool."

"I guess it doesn't matter if you dislike someone terribly, cause when something like this happens, then everyone seems to come together to offer love and support. Then nothing matters but that person."

"I agree. Grace. I've been thinking the very same thing and was talking to my parents about it before I came to get you."

"My heart aches for Brooke, and for her parents. Poor Brooke's parents—she's an only child. I can't imagine the pain and anguish they are experiencing at this time. She may be my Fake Blonde Clone nemesis, but she is still a human with feelings, and obviously with issues like all the rest of us." I sigh and turn toward Jake.

He takes me in his arms and kisses me like a passionate kiss.

Dang. I love this boy.

"Grace, I've said this before, and I mean it. You are as good-hearted a person as I've ever known."

I smile and say to him, "As are you, sweetie, as are you!"

"Well, I still feel I could have helped with this situation between you and Grace much more, but dang, she was so difficult to reason with! I don't know why!"

CHAPTER TWENTY-THREE

The radio was still on. We both sit back for a moment, still holding hands. If our brains had visual speech bubbles, there would have been so many popping up with so many different questions: *Why? How? What if? And on and on.*

I pull out the card I had chosen for Brooke. I open it still unsure as to what to write.

"What the heck do I write, Jake?"

"Ummm...."

"Exactly." I ponder for a few more minutes, then scribble out a brief message:

Brooke, I am so sorry. Please get well and I hope you wake up soon! Then, I think we should try to be friends.... Love Gracie Miller ☺

Jake reads what I wrote. "That's perfect." He writes on the card, too.

Brooke, get well soon, your friend, Jake Hansen"

I seal it up in an envelope. A tiny teardrop trickles down my cheek and ends up landing on the envelope, making a blob mark on the outside, as I turn it over to write Brooke's name on the front. Jake grabs the food cards, I've the card and flowers. Luckily, Costco has vases for sale too. They think of everything!

Jake takes my hand and we walk side by side from his car into the hospital's main doors. There's a slight breeze again today—aw, Spring. My favorite season! As we go through the entrance doors, I catch a whiff of spring flowers in the planters beside the doors. They tickle my senses with their fragrance and send waves of calm through my mind and body.

"Here we go!"

Jake grimaces, and we walk together toward the elevators.

I push the four button. We ride in silence again. This is a lot emotionally for everyone.

WE SEE JUSTIN SITTING ON THE BENCH. HE LOOKS BEDRAGGLED.

"Dude, you okay?" Jake asks kindly.

"I'm a little tired, ha ha."

"Uh, no offense, friend, but you need to go home and get some sleep." I put my hand on his shoulder.

"Yeah, gonna do that now that you both are here."

"Okay, go!" I point toward the elevators. Justin grabs his bag, says his goodbyes to the Marchants, and wearily walks to the elevators.

"Poor kid," Mr. Marchant says.

"He's so sweet to our Brookey," Ms. Marchant says sweetly. They both look exhausted, too.

"Hey," Jake starts to say, "let Grace and me stay here for a few hours with Brooke. You guys go home and catch a nap, how about?"

"Are you sure?" Ms. Marchant asks.

"Most definitely," I say. "We will see you both later on!"

They both smile a tired smile and grab their cell phones and bags and make the same weary walk to the elevators.

Jake and I grab the same two chairs from earlier and pull them softly over to Brooke's bedside. It may seem silly to be quiet when Brooke is in a coma, but you know, I feel I need to be reverent and respectful to her, even when she isn't awake.

Brooke still looks beautiful. Her tanned skin has yellowed bruise spots, though, and her hair is mussed, but still beautiful. Jake starts the conversation with her. The docs told us all to talk to Brooke—you just never know what the patients can hear.

"Hey, Brooke, it's Jake, and Gracie. We came back to visit with you again. We were here earlier this morning after you, uh, you came out of surgery…" His voice drifts lower and lower, so I chime in.

"Yeah, uh, Justin called us when this all went down, and, um we came right over. So, we both," I gesture at myself and Jake, "just want you to know that we're here for you, and, um, we, um, will both be back up when we can next week between school and work, so, so, um, I guess my question is, what the heck happened?"

"I think that's what I wanted to know too," Jake adds.

"I-I mean, we are both super sorry this happened, I mean it sucks so badly. We are so sorry that you're hurt and, um, that, you had a fight with your dad and all…." Now it was my turn to have my voice drift off somewhere.

I take Brooke's hand and Jake puts his hand on top of my hand, and we sit like this for a long while. Finally, I find my voice again.

"Brooke, when you wake up, I think we should start again—you, me, Jake, all of us. I think we can make this work, I mean, I hope we can." Jake looks at me and nods in agreement.

"Thank you both for coming by and sitting with our girl."

We both jump slightly. When did the Marchant's get back?

We stand quickly and walk out of Brooke's room.

"We were glad too. I hope you got to get cleaned up and rest up some."

"We did, and we thank you for allowing us to do that. Justin texted and said he will be back up for about an hour, then it's school tomorrow and…."

Her facial features darkened with instant sadness.

"Um, a lot of us have classes with Brooke, so when she wakes up, we can help her catch up or share our notes or whatever is needed."

"Thank you, Grace. I will call the high school tomorrow too, and have her classwork and homework saved, et cetera, too."

"See you soon, Mrs. Marchant." Jake says sweetly and then takes my hand and leads us both to the elevators.

I am really quiet on the elevator ride down.

"Gracie? What's up?"

"She doesn't even know who I am, Jake, Mrs. Marchant, I mean, not Brooke. But I guess, Brooke, too obvi," I mutter.

"I know, I know! It's so crazy. All of this!" Jake says, exasperated.

"Seriously! I just hope she will wake up, and soon. I guess I didn't hate her all that much, because my heart is aching for the Marchants and for Brooke, which means I'm not heartless."

"Gracie, you never have been heartless. She does have a lot of responsibility in this whole situation, too, but now we will just both have to start over with her like you said to her."

"Yeah, I guess that's all we can do." I sigh sadly.

We walk off of the elevator solemnly and then out into the moonlit sky. I realize as we near Jake's Jeep, that throughout our visit tonight, Jake has been more quiet than usual. I am concerned now and need to address it.

"You want to come back and hang at my house, Jake? I know it's late and all."

"Yes. I need to be with you right now. All of this is bringing back memories of my mother's accident. I need to be with you and your family, please."

"Wait, wait, what? Your mom was in an accident? Why didn't you say anything when I was blubbering about my dad?"

"Well, 'cause my mom lived and your dad died, so I felt stupid even wanting to mention it. Okay, I was ten years old, so I remember it well. She was so messed up. It was hard for me to even look at her face. She was in the hospital for about two months! I went to see her every day. It was a lot. Megan was six, so she came a few times, but it was really hard for her to see our mom like that. When she finally came home, it took her a good six months or so to be fully healed."

We reach his Jeep just as he finishes sharing this, and before getting in, I reach my arms around him and draw him to me in a hug. I want him to know how much I care for him and that I also need him just as much, and how I continue to like him more and more each day.

It is amazing how I feel about him. He has made my silly, young life complete. Jake hugs me back and we stand like that for a good five minutes. I can feel him breathing slowly against me. I lean up to kiss his cheek. I wiped away a stray tear from his face. My heart aches for him too!

"Oh, Jake! I am so sorry. I didn't even know this!"

"I chose to not tell you, because your dad died, and my mom didn't. It's not something I talk about very much. Meg was still little, so she wasn't as impacted. I knew too much as an almost-eleven-year-old. I mean thankfully, she healed completely, but going to the hospital was really hard and made me feel very little and vulnerable."

"I can only imagine."

Once we get in the car, I grab his hand and hold it close to me. He turns and smiles at me but is silent on the car ride to my house. I'm assuming his mind is churning with emotions, since I had had my own experience with the same type of feelings and emotions with my father's death. I decide to call Zac as we continue to drive, to let him know we are coming back and see if it was okay for Jake to stay for a bit-even though it's late.

"Hey, Zac."

"Hey Gracie, what's up?"

"Jake and I are coming back from seeing that girl, Brooke, at the hospital."

"Yeah. That's awful. I'm so sorry."

"Yeah, it's pretty awful. Is there any food left over from dinner?"

"Oh, yeah. Plenty. See you guys in a bit. Oh, Megan is still here, too, by the way. She wanted me to tell you guys."

"K. Cool. Thanks."

"Zac says there's plenty of food left over—yay, 'cause I am starved—and Meg's at our house still."

"Okay, thanks, Gracie." He holds my hand tighter as we approach my neighborhood.

Once at my house, we go right into the family room. Zac and Sarah are there, and Meg and Beth are playing a game on the floor. Mom is there, too, with Kenneth. It was a regular party at my house, and it was nearly eleven pm!

"Hey, sis, how was the visit? How does she look?" Beth's face has a questioning look as she asks this.

"It was okay. Despite being very banged up, she is still beautiful. This is the first time I could really see her for who she is though, too. No makeup. Just Brooke. She looks very peaceful. Jake and I sat by her and spoke with her. I held her hand, argh, it's all so sad. I just hope she wakes up and sooner than later, 'ya know?"

"It is really good of you guys to go up there, despite how things have gone between you all. Come have a seat. Sarah and I can get you some food." Zac motions to Sarah.

"Yeah, of course. Let us feed you both. Drinks?

"Thanks, Zac, thanks, Sarah. Just water for me."

"Ditto for me guys, thanks."

We sit on the couch, and I have Jake rest his head on my lap. I grab the book he bought for me on our first date. It has been a little crazy in my life for a few weeks, and I have not been able to get back to reading it. As I pick it up, a paper flutters out of the book and drops to the floor. I try to pick it up without disturbing Jake too much. He already is closing his eyes. It's a bookmark from the bookstore. But there is writing on it from Jake. It reads, "Thank you for going out with me. Have sweet dreams as you read this book before bed, and hopefully you will think of me as I will be thinking of you."

Oh, my gosh! That is so sweet! I run my fingers through Jake's hair. He looks up at me. I smile.

How did I get so lucky, to have found this gem of a guy, like really?

CHAPTER TWENTY-FOUR

He closes his eyes again. I pick up my book and begin to read. I feel Jake's weight shift and get heavier, meaning he's fallen asleep. I figure this is the best thing for him. I know how Zac gets sometimes with emotional things. They wear him out and not talking occurs when he's upset.

About fifteen minutes later, Zac and Sarah return with two plates and two water bottles. They take Jake's back since he's sleeping. I clean the plate. Dang, I guess I really was starving. I drink most of my water bottle, too, then get back to my book.

I must have dozed off, because it is mostly dark except for the corner light. when I open my eyes. No one is in the room with me, but I hear laughter from the kitchen. I put up my book, tucking in the bookmark tenderly. I drag myself off of the couch. My head suddenly hurts. I must have slept deeply, though short. I walk through the kitchen doorway. Everyone is at the table. Jake gets up and comes to me. He gives me a quick hug.

"Hey, sleeping beauty. You were out cold, so I let you take a snooze, too. Thanks for letting me rest, sweetie."

"Of course. Um, I found the bookmark in my book. So sweet." I place my hand tenderly on his cheek.

"Okay, you two, break it up. We all need to go to bed!"

"Thanks, Mom," I sassily say as I go to the table with Jake. Kenneth left a while ago.

"I'll take Sarah home and be right back. Here comes a weekday tomorrow, whether we're ready or not!" We all groan loudly and then burst out with laughter.

Jake and I usually hang at my house since his mom has come back, just to give his parents the time needed to work through things, Megan and Beth are always together. I love it. Jake and Meg fit in perfectly with us all. I always love when we're together. I just can't believe how happy everyone looks when we're with each other. Ugh. But then picturing Brooke lying in bed in a coma breaks through my rainbowy thoughts, and I groan to myself. Blast. I try to push it all out of my mind.

It's time for everyone to go now. Megan packs her stuff. Zac is back from taking Sarah home. And Jake and I embrace, our hearts hurting from past trauma and current sadness, and happy all at the same time because of the good things surrounding, and we need each other's affection to help us heal and to connect.

BROOKE HAS BEEN IN A COMA FOR ALMOST A MONTH. HER VITALS HAVE been consistent, but she has not shown many signs of waking, until today! It's nearly the end of the school year, and it feels legit like the days are flying by me—I can't even keep up—and before we know it, summer will be upon us. I keep up with Justin via texts and try to check in with him every few days. And then TODAY I receive a text from him saying that Brooke's eyes had fluttered early this morning her mom said! AND she squeezed her mom's hand in response to various questions she had asked her.

I text Jake to let him know of Brooke's progress from Justin, and also ask him if we can go up to the hospital when he comes over later. He, of course, says yes. Sigh. Jake is such a good person.

It's late Thursday afternoon. I have just finished my shift for the day at Sicily's, make it home quickly so I can shower and dress before Jake is due to come over in about an hour.

Jake and I have gone shopping over the past few months together, and I have purchased some new clothes that I really like—Jake is *really* good at shopping for a dude—and I am feeling more confident, so the combination of his help and my confidence has given me quite the excellent wardrobe.

I pull on a patterned sundress with pinks and yellows in it and throw on a cap-sleeved pink tee under it. I slip on my new pink sandals, too. I get a text from Jake that he is on his way. I pop into my mom's office, since I had heard her come in from going to the store, while I was getting ready.

"Hey, Mom, guess what? I just got a text from Justin. Brooke squeezed her mom's hand multiple times and her eyes fluttered, too!"

"Oh, Grace, that is excellent news! Oh, thank goodness!" She is so excited, even her face lights up.

"Justin is already at the hospital, so Jake and I are wanting to go over to the hospital and visit her tonight, if that's okay with you?"

"Sure, honey, of course! You guys definitely need to go and see her. Oh, I sure hope she will really wake up. I can't even imagine how difficult this has been for Brooke's parents. Ugh. It breaks my heart for them all."

"Agreed. I mean, to see her there every day in front of you, just lying there—but not to actually "be there" is horrible! Comas are the strangest to me. I am so glad she's finally making some movement. I'll fill you in more on the details when I'm back later tonight, okay?"

"Sounds great. Love you, sweetie!" She blows me a kiss.

I close her office door just as Jake texts that he's here. I grab a sweater—it is always cold in the hospital—and make sure to lock the front door after I shut it. I jump into Jake's Jeep (he has the door open for me—so sweet) and he softly kisses my cheek and closes the door. I think my heart will always flutter any time he kisses me!

I grab his hand and we drive in silence. My mind drifts as we drive to the hospital. I feel discombobulated with the news of Brooke showing signs of life. I feel happy for her and her parents, of course, but then I feel a sense of terror wash over me that reminds me when she wakes up she could be right back to her old mean girl crap to me. I sincerely hope that some sort of miracle has transpired and that while being in the coma, Brooke might have had a complete change of heart?!

Hey! I can hope and wish and hope some more, can't I?

"Yeah, right!" I mumble under my breath.

"What's up Gracie? You okay?" We arrive at the hospital and as Jake is searching for a parking spot he adds, "I find that I am super happy for Brooke and her parents. And then on the flip side, I am very concerned that she'll be the same mean girl that she's been all year long. I just don't know if we can both handle that emotionality, 'ya know?"

"Ha, Jake! That is funny you are thinking that, 'cause I am thinking that very same thing right now." How does he always know I need to talk about things that are occupying my mind? Sheesh!

"Also, Grace, before we go in, I've been wanting to tell you something. I want to be straight with you and tell you more about us—uh, Brooke and me—when we both lived in California."

Jake puts the Jeep in park but leaves the air on. The Texas weather is already hot and humid. Summer is comin'. He turns toward me.

I look at him and suddenly feel a chill come over me. *What is he going to tell me?* I have an icky feeling come over me. Jake notices my face has changed color and immediately grabs my hand.

"Gracie, I promise you it's not what you think. In fact, it's the opposite of what you will expect me to tell you. I promise."

I blow out a long breath. "Okay, then. Tell me." I look at him and he begins to unravel the details.

"It was two years ago, so freshman and sophomore years. As you know, Meg and I were born and raised in California until we moved here. Well, the school year had just started, like maybe just a few days, and one day, in walks Brooke. She actually wasn't as all dolled up like she is now. She was really quiet and very plain looking. Pretty, but plain and not decked out to the nines, as the saying goes. So, she comes into one of my classes and then she ends up being in a few other of my classes too. For the first year she was just chill and was a good student and all. Then the next year, this other new girl moves in and befriends Brooke, and it was as if I was watching *Mean Girls* or *Clueless* but in real time and in real life. She went from plain Jane to over-the-top Brooke. And she gained more confidence too. She changed her hair, her wardrobe, all of her! It was crazy to watch. And then—"

He sighs a deep sigh. "Then, for some reason, she starts to zero in on me. She literally would try and be by me whenever she could. She'd grab my arm and giggle. She'd try and whisper in my ear. She'd ask me for rides home and so on and so forth. You get the point. You see how she is. It was awful. It drove me nuts and one day, I'd had it and was going to have a little talk with her when her dad came to school and checked her out and she was gone. At the time I had no idea why. But boy, was I happy and relieved. That was a really long year. I later found out her dad had some shady business dealings or something like that and they had to move quickly. Not sure where she went. And I still can't believe she ended up here, of all the dang places to move to!"

"Oh, my gracious. That's crazy! I wonder why people change like that? Like what provoked such a change? And why she pursued you so aggressively—dang—it is craziness! And of all the places for her to move to? What are the odds?"

"Yeah, for real. Imagine how I felt the day she walks into our English class! I almost got up and left, and Gracie, please know that you needn't worry about her. Ever. She's never been my type and never will be. Ever!" And with those words, he leans over and pulls me in for a hug. We stay like that for what seemed like five minutes. Then he pulls away and kisses me.

We're at the elevators. I push floor three—my hand is trembling—so Jake grabs my hand.

"No matter what, we've made the best choice. We've been kind. We've been supportive. We've been here for Justin and for Brooke's parents."

"True." I let out a huge breath. The door opens.

"Here we go!" We walk methodically toward Brooke's room. We see Justin first, then Brooke's parents. They're all chatting with a doctor. As we approach them all, Justin breaks away and literally runs toward us excitedly.

"She's fully awake! She's talking, she's smiling! It's a miracle!"

He has tears in his eyes. I go toward him, and we embrace.

"I could not be happier. For real. It is a miracle!"

Jake gives Justin a hug too.

"Guys, I, um, I just want to thank you for being so supportive this whole month," he runs his hand through his curly, mussed up hair, and continues. "And I'm not unaware of how Brooke has been to you specifically, Gracie, since she moved her. You may not believe this, but Brooke never treated me like that when we were together, which is why I know she has it in her to be nice—okay, well, nicer." His words seem to linger mid-air. There's a strange silence for a minute or so, then I decide I better say something.

"Um, well, yeah, it's been pretty bad for me, well, more like a suck-fest for me since she moved here. I've hated it. And if it wasn't for Jake, I wouldn't have been able to survive her cruelty! I appreciate you sharing this with me though, and I hope and pray and hope again, that Brooke won't be her old self." I state this resolutely.

"Me too," Jake states matter-of-factly.

"Me too, guys, me too. I mean, so far, she's been pretty groggy and just has been asking what happened to her and why she's in the hospital. So that's good I guess?"

"Yes, it is," Jake and I say this together.

We all three walk toward Brooke's room.

Argh-I hope I can do this.

CHAPTER TWENTY-FIVE

rooke and I lock eyes. We stay like this for a couple seconds, and then, her face breaks into a beautiful smile. I mean her eyes even sparkle.

"Gracie! Jake! Oh my gosh! You're here? Are you here to see me?"

Jake and I look at each other and then look back at Brooke and nod our heads.

"Come in! Come in!" Brooke is exuberant.

Wow.

We walk in and flank her bed on each side. Justin is on her left side. I stand by him. Jake moves to her other side. Her parents are still talking to the doctor.

"You guys! I can't believe you're all here!" She takes our hands.

Okay, woah, I'm gonna try to NOT freak out right now. Did Brooke hit her head THAT hard? Okay that's not nice, but what the?

"Brooke! I can't believe you're awake! Holy moly." This is all I can think to say.

"Me too!" Jake says kindly..

"Oh, I am *so* happy!" Justin is beaming from ear to ear.

"Guys! I can't believe I was in a freakin' coma for a month!" She sits up to say this and then lies back again.

"Neither can we!" We all say this in agreement.

"It was really long." Justin grabs Brooke's hand. He sniffs. She grips his hand.

"I can't even believe how much of life I've missed! School, my parents, you guys…." She stops abruptly and sniffs, too. Tiny tears appear in the corners of her beautiful, clear, blue eyes.

"I wonder if you guys would mind if I talk with Gracie—alone—for a bit?" She has a pleading expression.

"Sure," Jake says low and hesitantly. He stares at me.

I mouth to him, "I will be okay."

"Of course, Brooke," Justin says happily.

The boys walk out. Jake immediately turns around and watches us both from outside of her room and through the glass.

"Gracie? Grab the chair and pull it over, please."

I do so. My heart is beating so fast. I don't even know what is going to happen right now, but if nightmares do come true, this would be mine. I sit down. Her beautiful face turns toward me. Her hair is still messy, and her poor face has now yellow bruise spots, but she is and always will be like a porcelain doll—flawlessly beautiful.

"Gracie," she begins softly and says my name deliberately. "Gracie, I know you must be terrified right now."

"Not gonna lie, Brooke, but yes, I sure am."

"Right, and yes, you should be." She closes her eyes for a few seconds.

"Hey, if you're tired, we can talk later."

"No, no, I'm okay. I need to do this. I must say this to you." She swallows.

"You didn't ever deserve the way I treated you. No one deserves it, but you especially. You're nothing but nice! You put up with me for way too long. I just, I am just so sorry, Gracie." She looks at me with tenderness.

Ummmm, like I didn't know her face could show this emotion.

"I, um—" I start to say something, but Brooke cuts me off.

"I need to finish saying all of this then I will take a nap." She smiles sweetly at me.

"Look, I was a hideous, jerky person to you and sometimes to Jake. Why? You've probably asked this question a million times to yourself. And who can blame you? I would have asked myself that question too. Well, here it is. I thought that since I reinvented myself—I'm sure Jake filled you in on what I was like in Cali—well, it turned out that I was pretty. Really pretty, and I could use that to my advantage, and boys did I. A lot."

I raise my eyebrows questioningly, and I am sure my face looks surprised.

"Yeah, I know, pretty lame and stupid. I know. Well, as I continued to use people and boss people and most of all, the response I got from boys and men, that gave me power. I felt invincible, and I just decided to buy into that and I became more and more mean. Since I was pretty, people did stuff I asked them too. Girls and guys alike. My parents always told me I was pretty and the best, and all that stuff, yada, yada. Anyways, when I was in my coma, I had some weird out of body experiences. It was crazy! And you know what? Everything was the opposite. I was on the other end and this awful girl—umm, she actually looked like you—well, she treated me awfully. Mean, rude, unkind you name it, she did it to me. This dream came to me I guess every night until just before I woke up, and then the dream switched, and it was me being the mean girl to you and I could feel how it felt to be treated like I treated you. I could feel it. It was intense, the pain as I was saying these things to you as if I was speaking to myself. It was so weird. But it is obviously what I needed to wake myself up from my reverie of cruelty I'd sunk into for years and years."

I am stunned. Shocked. My mouth is slightly ajar, I think.

She continues. "And this morning when I woke up, I knew it was time for a huge soul overhaul. And that I had to tell you all of this before, well, before I saw you again and you would walk the other way knowing that I'd just continue to treat you hideously."

We look down for a bit then look up at each other.

"Oh, wait!" This is me speaking now. "The night you crashed, did you know you started to text me?" I ask her questioningly.

"Ugh, I was hoping it hadn't gone through. I was gonna give you a snarky text because it had been a while, when all of a sudden, I hit some curve and that's all I remember." She sighs and then sniffs. She has tears coming down her face now. I look around and for a box of Kleenex on one of the counters. I grab it and give it to her. She pulls a few out and wipes her eyes and blows her nose.

"Well, I obviously am horrified this happened to you, but kind of glad I never got your mean text!" She looks at me and we burst into laughter. Us! Together!

I cannot believe this is happening, but I am so stoked. So happy. So relieved. Miracles DO happen!

As we're laughing, I look over at Jake through the window. He's got the cutest smile on his beautiful face and gives me a thumbs up. I return the thumbs up, and Brooke and I continue to talk for quite a while.

I walk out of the room. My facial expression must show how I'm feeling right now because I'm snapped out of my reverie with these words:

"Wanna get a Braum's burger before I drop you home? Gracie? Hellooooo?"

"Ummm what?" I can't help but laugh!

"Oh my gosh! I'm so sorry. I think I was in some sort of dream state. Pinch me. Quickly! Am I awake?"

We both laugh. It feels good. The stress that built up in us both before visiting with Brooke was palpable!

"Yes please! I'm starving!"

"Done!"

We continue to laugh and talk as Jake drives us to Braum's. It's one of our fave spots to eat.

Ten minutes later, we are parked in my driveway munching and talking.

"I am still in shock about the whole Brooke sitch. I mean who knew?"

"For real. Wow. I'm in shock too. I didn't know if he had it in her to allow herself to be who I knew she once was. Ya know?"

"Completely. What an ordeal. I never would ever wish what

happened to Brooke on anyone, but I'm sure not gonna lie. Best change of heart story ever!"

"Right? Amazing. And with almost three weeks of school left!"

"Ugh. Poor Brooke. What will she do now having missed more than a month of school?"

"Yeah, that sucks. She's smart, so I wonder if she could have a few unit quizzes given to her and she just study for those and her teachers could see how she does?"

"Hmmm. Not a bad idea. Maybe we should suggest she ask someone about that idea. Are you cool if I share the info with Brooke?"

"Of course! Good idea."

Wrapping up junior year, I have a lot of feels. I'm excited. I'm nervous. Senior year is just three months away. Which means the start of applying to colleges. And what will Jake and I do? Zac and Sarah will be leaving at the end of this summer. Which already breaks my heart. But I know it needs to happen. Then, Mom♥ and Kenneth are going to get married at the end of this month of May. And they have decided to make it a destination wedding in Hawaii. So, all of us are going. Even Jake and his family.

His mom, Penelope, and his dad, are doing great. It seems like everything is back together for them now. Which makes me happy. And obviously, Jake and Megan are both just overjoyed. Sent the text to Brooke with Jake's idea. I'm sure hoping her teachers can cooperate with her. At least she is very intelligent. Even if she acting like a bimbo head before she got into her crash. At least I know she can handle studying and passing the unit test, if she's able to do such a thing. Two weeks left of school, it's finals time. Which means Jake and I are studying together every single day. Which I never complain about being able to be with Jake whenever I can.

I took a couple weeks off from work as to Jake so we could study and prepare for the fun Hawaiian destination wedding for my mom and Kenneth. I still can't believe that she's going to get remarried. But I'm happy about it. Not in a bad way. Just the fact that this is all happening. That it's almost four years since my dad's been gone and we've changed a lot. There's been good times, hard times, and sad times. But now it seems like we're all kind of on the up and up. Which is a wonderful feeling for myself, Beth, Zac, and most of all, Mom♥.

Graduation day came and went for Zac and Sarah. Oh! They both got into UT Austin, so that's amaze. I am going to be so sad when Zac moves out. I mean I know we both have significant others, but he is my bestest friend and bro, well, my only bro. He and Sarah will take off in July. And now it's just one week until Mom and Kenneth's wedding day and our trip to Hawaii with everyone!

I still can't believe all that happened. It's been a whirlwind of activities. Life. Love. Friendship. You name it and it's happened! Love is def in the air in the Miller family! Well, except Beth, but she has her BFF, and this is about the happiest we have all been in four years. It feels good. I just hope everything can stay like this forever, ha ha, and that I could just freeze time and we just stay in our happy little bubble we are in right now!

How's Brooke, you ask? Ready for the answer?! Fabulous. We all hang together every day! Brooke and Justin. Jake and me. Zac and Sarah. Kenneth and Mom and Beth and Megan. And! Brooke and Justin are coming with us too, to the wedding!

'I can't believe we all fly out tomorrow. Can u?'

'For real. So stoked.'

'Right?? Can't wait to be done and pack.'

I am texting Jake from my break during work. My Saturday shift is short, so Jake and I are coordinating with Beth and Meg to do some last-minute shopping before we all fly out. Jake didn't have to work at Joe's today, but he did at the house—cleaning, taking Meg where she needed, etc. And Brooke and Justin have some family stuff, so we will see them at the airport. Our flights leave at 11:30 am. It's a good eight-hour flight. Ugh. But worth it, obvi, since it's to Hawaii. Duh.

'Gotta go.'

'K. C u at your house.'

The rest of my shift flies by, as always on a Saturday. Julie and Shawn have done a great job with their PR for Sicily's Take n' Bake Pizza, so it is always busy. Julie has three more weeks until their son (it will be their third boy!) is to be born, so they recently hired her younger sister, Mary Catherine, to help manage for the next while and get trained before the baby is born and then Mary Catherine will take over after. Julie is going to stay home with the baby for a few years since her older boys are in elementary school.

"Girl! You're done. Go have fun!"

"Thanks Julie! See y'all in two weeks. And I'll def send pics!"

"You better!" She winks at me. "Great work as always. Say hi to Jake," Julie says with a sassy smile.

"Oh, I will!" I retort sarcastically

"Have so much fun!"

We hug and I turn and wave as I push the door open. Man, oh, man, how I love Julie. As I walk out into the bright, warm sunshine, I stop. I see Jake.

Wait, what? He's like a knight in shining armor, okay, standing by his shiny Jeep.

"Hey! You're here?"

I smile as I walk toward him. My heart pitter-patters. It's like that scene in *Sixteen Candles* at the end when Jake is standing by the car waiting for Molly Ringwald. It's so freaking romantic, and now I'm walking to my hot Jake.

"Surprise! I had Zac help me take Old Blue to your house so I could pick you up myself."

I'm at his car. Standing in front of him. He's so beautiful. Dang. I smile as he pulls me into a hug. I reciprocate and hug him back.

We hug for a few minutes. Then he pulls back and brings me close to kiss me. I close my eyes.

"I missed you today," he says into my ear and then kisses me again.

I feel as if I'm floating in a bubble. "I always miss you."

He kisses me once more and takes my hand and leads me to the passenger door. I hop in. Shut the door and then turn toward him.

"I am the luckiest girl to have you in my life. I never think I deserve you though." I blush and lower my gaze.

"Well, funny you say that, cause I feel the same way. How did I get so lucky to find you?"

We lock eyes. He pulls me close and kisses me tenderly on the lips. I close my eyes again.

"Hawaii is going to be marvelous with you, Gracie."

"Any day anywhere is marvelous with you, Jake," I whisper, and I kiss him again.

A NOTE FROM THE AUTHOR

This story stems from my real-life experiences with the so-called popular girls and boys in middle school and high school who were so mean to me! It was awful. I had my clothes stolen in eighth grade. I was mocked daily all through seventh grade for my knock off topsiders and clothing. I was rejected by a group of girls in my early morning scripture class because I looked very different and weird (to be fair I'd just come from living for a year abroad in Scotland) so I had a perm and was as thin as a stick! Even in college, there was this one girl from back East who just couldn't handle that I was a Cali girl who wore white whenever I wanted. She always said to me, "You don't wear white after September." Ummm what? Do you know where I come from? Anyways, it took me a long while to deal with my hurt feelings and low self-esteem issues. It was when I went off to college that I decided to do a thing. I reinvented myself: changed my hair, my wardrobe and tried to be friendly, fun, and popular. BUT, I was never, ever mean. I made sure of that and still do this to this day. NO ONE needs to feel that they are less than someone else. Especially when it comes to what they wear. How they choose to do their hair. Their makeup etc. This is a very personal choice and one that no one needs to have others weighing in on by sharing their personal opinions. I chose to write about a popular girl who actually does not win the attractive guy-but the middle of the road girl does instead. To me, this scenario seems more realistic to me. I did make another change: the mean girl has a change of heart which adds a kinder element to this story. And, again in my opinion, I'm hoping this is more realistic as life goes, than the pretty, popular girl always getting the hot, popular guy. I mean, sure this happens, and probs a lot, but I felt that I'd rather tell my story this way. I will never forget the way those mean girls made me feel-never-and I have wanted to express these sentiments in my writing for many years. And now I am via *The Trouble with Blondie*. I hope you enjoyed it!